Rod of

Also by John W Green:

Growing Up in Lee-on-the-Solent

Exploring the History of Lee-on-the-Solent
    (co-authored with Robin Money)

Rod of Moses

John W Green

CHAPLIN BOOKS

www.chaplinbooks.co.uk

First published in 2016 by Chaplin Books
Copyright © John W Green

ISBN: 978-1-911105-04-6

The moral right of John W Green to be identified as the author of this work has been asserted in accordance with the Copyright, Designs and Patents Act of 1988.

All rights reserved. No part of this publication may be reproduced, stored in any retrieval system or transmitted in any form or by any means, electronic, mechanical, photocopying, recording or otherwise, without the prior written permission of the copyright holder for which application should be addressed in the first instance to the publishers. No liability shall be attached to the author, the copyright holder or the publishers for loss or damage of any nature suffered as a result of the reliance on the reproduction of any of the contents of this publication or any errors or omissions in the contents.

A CIP catalogue record for this book is available from The British Library

Design by Michael Walsh at The Better Book Company

Printed by Imprint Digital

Chaplin Books
1 Eliza Place
Gosport PO12 4UN
Tel: 023 9252 9020
www.chaplinbooks.co.uk

Yesterday upon the stair
I met a man that wasn't there
He wasn't there again today
I wish I wish he'd go away

William Hughes Mearns

Jack went inside the ruin. He had a good look round and decided that the side in the shade would be the best place to dig the latrine. Apart from the shade, the remains of the wall would also afford some privacy. There was a shrub growing in the corner, so he decided to dig midway along that wall.

On the second jab of the shovel he hit wood. *'Well it can't be floorboards,'* he thought. *'The houses only have mud or stone floors.'* He scraped the soil off the wood and it became apparent that it was the top of a box. He dug all around it and lifted it out of the hole that he'd now made. It was about four feet long, eight inches wide and eight inches deep. Maybe someone had buried a rifle or a large sword? Maybe it was buried treasure? He levered off the top of the box with the edge of the shovel. He figured he had made enough mistakes for one day so he didn't put his hand into the box to find out what treasure was hidden in it. *'Probably crawling with snakes or scorpions,'* he thought, remembering how every morning it was standard practice to check boots and socks before putting them on, to make sure that there were no venomous temporary lodgers hiding in them, having a siesta. He took out a match and lit it so that he could see what the box contained. No snakes or unpleasant creepy-crawlies and disappointingly no precious stones reflecting their presence back at him – no gold coins, not even a sword or a gun. The only thing in the box was an old stick, which had what looked like Arabic writing carved on it. There were a few bits of yellowed paper stuck to the stick and a square piece of wax with some sort of imprint on it, half attached to one of the pieces of paper. Jack carefully pulled the stick from the box, gave it a cursory inspection, threw it to one side, then continued digging the latrine.

CHAPTER ONE

Shuffling into a more comfortable position in the relative luxury of the third-class railway seat, Jack took a closer look at his travelling companions. Opposite was a young man probably about the same age as him – eighteen or nineteen – but his fresh complexion, accentuated by his black hair, contrasted so markedly with Jack's weather-beaten features that it made the traveller opposite look almost like a schoolboy.

'Simmer down lad,' thought Jack as he watched the young man fidget nervously, continually adjusting the position of his hands – their smooth skin and carefully cut nails revealed that he wasn't a manual worker – along the edges of the journal which he was half hiding behind and half reading. The magazine had pictures of airplanes on its cover.

Next to the young man sat a rather dispirited looking couple. The man was perhaps four or five years older than Jack and was wearing an old army greatcoat and an old army face, with the ugly scar of a shrapnel wound down one side of it. He was sitting totally motionless and from the look on his face Jack had the impression that his mind was focussed unwillingly on memories he would much rather forget. Alongside the ex-soldier was his wife, who looked to be about six months gone. She, like the young man, was fidgeting nervously. She wore a worried look in the same way that many people would wear an old familiar scarf to protect them from a cold wind. Jack guessed that she was about twenty-two but the frown made her look much older. It was easy to see that when she'd been a bit younger and less worried she had been really pretty.

The couple's brown paper parcel luggage, down-at-heel shoes, worn-out clothes and worn-out faces told all there was to tell of the poverty and hard times that they were enduring. *'It definitely hasn't turned out to be a land fit for bloody heroes,'* thought Jack as they all sat in silence – the silence of travellers. He couldn't help but contrast the appearance of the couple with that of the young man with his too neatly pressed trousers, carefully folded raincoat and neatly tied tie, and the obviously new shoes.

Shortly after boarding the train Jack had opened the window of the door to look out. He didn't know why; there certainly wasn't anyone to see him off and he no longer felt any real attachment for Sheffield – in fact he was quite glad to see the back of the place. Before sitting down he'd closed the window, but had inadvertently left a small gap at the top. Soon after they were underway the train entered a long tunnel and the compartment filled with a dirty yellow, sulphurous smoke. Jack leapt to his feet, grabbed the large leather strap and pulled it down so sharply that the window shot to the top with such a force that it nearly smashed the glass.

'Bloody hell!' he exclaimed. 'Sorry about that – it nearly gassed us all.'

'Don't worry, mate. No damage done and that's nothing like gas,' said the ex-soldier. 'I could tell you a thing or two about gas, it's ...' The sentence died as the haunted look once again took charge of his face.

'No, everything is alright,' added the young man. The worried wife said nothing, but an attempt at a small smile signalled that she agreed. The ice and the silence had been broken – conversation started and began to feed upon itself, eagerly gathering in strength.

'Where you off to then, mate?' 'Greatcoat' asked Jack.

'Well I've had an almighty row with me Old Man. I've been on the trawlers out of Grimsby for a while – up in the Arctic – but I've had enough of that, so I'm off to London to see if I can make a go of it down there.'

'What about the steel works – couldn't you get a job there?' asked Greatcoat.

'I did two years there after I left school. That was what the row was about – he wanted me to go back and I didn't want to.'

'We're off to Canterbury, but I've heard Welwyn Garden City is very nice,' chipped in Mrs Greatcoat, suddenly eager not to be left out of the conversation.

The surprised look on the young man's face when Jack was talking about the row with his Old Man was apparent. Jack thought the lad probably came from the kind of house where he wasn't allowed even to mildly disagree with his father, let alone have a row with him.

'What's your name then, young 'un?' said Greatcoat to the lad. 'Where are you off to?'

The lad started.

'Sorry, I was miles away. I'm David White and I'm going to London to join the RAF. It was my father's idea.'

Then eagerly he began to relate some of the stories that his father had told him. All the conversation that had been bottled-up inside suddenly was set free, and it became clear that he was good with words. He held them captivated for quite some time.

A little later, Mr and Mrs Greatcoat – now revealed to be called George and Esme – insisted on sharing their sandwiches with Jack and David. They were just finishing them as the train pulled into Nottingham station. Before the train had completely stopped Jack opened the door and jumped on to the platform.

'Shan't be a minute – keep my seat,' he called out. With that, he headed off in the direction of the waiting room. The door had been slammed shut and the rear guard had just blown his whistle when Jack appeared outside the carriage door, gesturing with his head for them to open the door. David nervously obliged and Jack jumped into the compartment carrying four mugs of tea. George slammed the door shut just as the train jerked into motion.

'We were sure that you'd missed it,' said Esme, looking more worried than ever.

'How did you manage to do that without spilling it all?' asked David, suitably impressed.

'Oh, you soon learn that trick at sea,' said Jack, smiling and passing round the LNER cups, pleased to be able to repay his companions' kindness. The tea went down very well.

As they put down their empty cups, the corridor door was abruptly pushed open by the rear guard, a tallish man with an officious bearing, a thin pencil moustache and a thin pencil face.

'Who opened that door after I had blown my whistle?'

David looked pale and frightened, but before he could say anything Jack was on his feet.

'I opened it, guard. There was a crowd at the buffet so it took me longer than I expected. Sorry – I didn't mean to cause any problems for you.'

The guard put on a self-satisfied sneer. 'Don't you realise, you young whippersnapper, that you were breaking railway regulations? This is a very serious breach of the rules and these cups here ...'

Jack interrupted him. 'I did say sorry, guard.'

'Well for your information, sorry is not good enough.' He prepared to start once again.

Jack, now flushed with anger, brushed past him into the corridor, turned and snapped:

'Thee get tha sen out here!' in his anger momentarily reverting to the dialect that he'd grown up with. Jack abruptly slammed the door shut behind the guard, who turned to glower at him. When he caught Jack's eye, he received a very nasty shock – a terrifying metamorphosis had taken place. This was very different to the young man that he'd been ticking off in the compartment. Those penetrating blue eyes were as cold as the ice in the Arctic where Jack had spent so much time during his formative years. Although the guard stood head and shoulders above him, it was as though their roles had been reversed. The guard turned quite pale. From the impressive width of Jack's shoulders it was easy to visualise the powerful arms and torso beneath the dark blue seaman's jumper that he was wearing – he'd been described by some of his shipmates as being 'built like a small brick shithouse.'

Now it was Jack's turn. In his time at sea he'd learnt quite a few choice variations of the English language – he'd been taught by well-practised experts.

'Now listen here, you pig-shit of an excuse for a man,' Jack began, his voice with the cutting edge of a polar wind. 'I left the train to get cups of tea for my friends in there. In case you haven't noticed, one of them's a woman who's in the family way and her husband is an ex-soldier – unlike yourself – who's spent years of his bloody life fighting and getting wounded for the effing likes of you. They don't need any jumped-up bugger trying to throw his weight around upsetting them and making an almighty bloody fuss over a pissing little thing like opening a door.'

Jack continued uninterrupted and uninterruptable for several minutes, his language becoming progressively more Anglo-Saxon.

The guard's thin lips became tight and white at the edges, his jaw muscles making small convulsing bulges near his ears and his cheeks taking on a purple tinge. Nobody talked to him like this. He would not have it – but he did and he kept silent. For the first time in his life he was completely intimidated – even the Head Stationmaster didn't frighten him this much. It was the eyes of the young man, his voice and the way that he held himself, the very essence of fearless and aggressive strength ... but most of all it was the eyes.

In a moment of courage the guard started to say, in a conciliatory tone: 'Well sir, I had waved my flag and ...' He was cut short by a look from Jack that sent a chill through him, making him wish that he'd kept quiet.

'You can take your flag and stick it up your arse for all I care, so piss off and crawl back into your hole.' With that Jack turned and re-entered the compartment. The guard didn't follow, but returned to the rear guard's van, to brood and think of all the quick answers that he should have made – but in his heart of hearts he knew that he would not have dared.

For a while after the confrontation in the corridor, the atmosphere in the compartment was very strained and subdued but before the train was halfway to London they were busily chatting once again. *'And what's tha going to do now?'* His Old Man's words met, mingled and merged with a chance remark of David's and sowed the seeds of an idea in Jack's mind and the seed of his future with it.

How many lives at some time or another have been changed by a chance remark, or just a single word? Probably most – the capricious nature of fate cannot be denied and so it was for Jack. Although when he looked back he could not be sure which of David's comments it had been that formed the pivotal point in his life, Jack was fairly certain that it must have been something that David had said about working in hot places. That, without doubt, had more appeal than the thought of spending more time in those bitterly cold Arctic waters. Four years of sailing to the fishing grounds had been hard, very hard, and he'd definitely had enough, even if the chance of finding another berth occurred. He'd become a first-rate seaman – a leading hand – and maybe he might have made skipper in ten years, that is if he lived that long. Every winter some poor sods didn't return from the 'fishing grounds', and Jack had no intention of joining the numbers of those lost at sea.

'It sounds as if joining the RAF might suit me.' This remark of Jack's was the only stimulus that David needed – certainly no recruiting Sergeant could have extolled the virtues of a life in the RAF more eloquently or persuasively. During one of David's more dramatic accounts of a desert battle involving the air-force, George chipped in with an urgent note of caution.

'Easy on, young 'un – fighting ain't fun at all, not when all them bullets and shells is whizzing round and you're not sure if the next one's got your name on it. All of them who tells you how good it is ain't never seen what it's really like. Maybe up in them airplanes it's alright, but on the ground it's bloody awful. Oh! Sorry, Es,' he added quickly, turning to his wife. 'She don't like me talking about the war, and she don't like me swearing. I gets to dreaming about it – well it's more like nightmares to tell the truth.'

'I hope she didn't hear me in the corridor,' thought Jack. She had, but she was secretly glad that someone had stood up for her and George. It was a long time since she had felt that anyone was on their side.

David continued, using less lurid descriptions. He was telling them about some of the attacks on the Mad Mullah's bands in Somaliland by a Wing Commander Bowhill, when Esme interrupted him.

'Sounds like the adventures of Lawrence of Arabia,' she said. 'Was it in the same place?'

David was visibly disappointed that his own tale was not captivating enough, but he diplomatically told her that it was somewhere near there. She could see that he'd missed the point of her asking the question, so she quickly said: 'Oh! Don't think that your story ain't exciting enough – it is, but we used to hear so much about Lawrence.'

He seemed mollified and continued. In fact he continued enthusiastically for quite some time, but clearly felt that he was then hogging the conversation, so politely stopped to let others have their say. Jack got the impression that David had many more tales about the RAF still to tell.

George started to tell them about what had been happening to himself and Esme: 'Of course it was 'good old George' when I got back from the war, but not good enough for me to get me old job back. I managed to get a few odd jobs here and there, but not the work that I used to do, and the money's been very poor – things have been pretty tough.'

'I know what you mean, George,' said Jack, remembering the difficulties that his family were enduring. George was anxious to continue his story and Jack could see this ...

'So you were saying, George?'

'Oh yes, well, Es and me got engaged before I went off to join Kitchener's Army, but we waited until after the war before we got married. With so little money coming in we haven't been able to set up our own home yet, and have a real married life, if you know what I mean.' David clearly didn't, but of course Jack did.

'You see, we've been living with Es's mum and dad, and although they've been very good to us it's not the same as having your own place. Anyhow, things are on the up-and-up now.' His face brightened as he went on to tell of their recent chance of a change in their fortunes. 'I've managed to get this job on a farm near Blean, not far from Canterbury, as a stockman. You see, that's the work I'm used to.'

'And a cottage goes with the job,' added Esme, her smiling face indicated how important this was to her.

'Only just in time, love. I expect you've noticed that me

missus is expecting.' He smiled and Esme blushed a little, and for a short while, her face lost some of its worried look. She took George's comments as a cue for her to take up the story.

'It's due in just under three months.'

There was a lull in the conversation.

'You must come and see us, if you can, after the baby's born. We would like that, we would be ever so pleased to see you, wouldn't we, George?'

He smiled and nodded his agreement.

'Here, George!' said Esme, taking a used envelope from a Lipton's brown paper carrier bag by her feet. 'Put our new address on that for Jack and David.'

George rummaged in the pocket of his greatcoat and eventually produced the stub of an indelible pencil. Wetting the tip, he printed with painstaking care, sticking his purple-tipped tongue out of the corner of his mouth as he wrote, in a rather childlike hand, the address to which they were heading.

David took the envelope from George.

'We would like very much to come and see you and the baby if we get the chance. Wouldn't we, Jack?'

It was Jack's turn to nod an agreement, but it had not escaped his notice that David was assuming that the two of them would be together at this future date. Had his face given away what he'd been thinking? A bit unlikely, thought Jack, as he recalled one of his earlier nicknames – 'old poker face.'

By the time they'd reached London, Jack had agreed to go to Burlington Gardens with David so that he could find out a bit more about the RAF. Jack was no wide-eyed youngster easily persuaded by romantic tales, but he did realise that when all the layers of excited description were peeled from what David had said, at the heart there appeared to be a pretty good prospect of a satisfying job, and he certainly liked the sound of it. Nevertheless he would need more information before he made up his mind. One impulsive decision was enough for one day.

George suggested to Jack that he should think about it very carefully.

'You want to go easy, Jack. Service life ain't all fun and games,' he said.

David looked quite downcast at this comment but didn't

say anything. Shortly after this the train pulled into Kings Cross station and they all hastily gathered-up their luggage and disembarked. Jack and David said cheerio to George and Esme and promised to try to visit them after their baby was born. The two pairs waved to each other as they set off on their separate ways, George and Esme to the farm near Canterbury, Jack and David into the unknown.

CHAPTER TWO

'Well! Tell me about this Queen of Sheba and her country,' Solomon demanded of the envoy who had just returned from the South. Akil proceeded to give Solomon a detailed description of what he had seen in Sheba. As usual it was difficult to follow a line of thought when giving a report to the King because he constantly interrupted. Akil was well aware that he owed his status in the community to the patronage of the King, so he suffered it silently. Not only that, he was also aware that it was not a good idea to upset Solomon because he was not averse to 'dispose' of those who questioned the way that he did things.

Akil continued to describe what he had seen – a land rich in spices and where gold and precious stones were mined.

'The Queen also rules over a land across the sea in the east called Ophir, from where they get a great deal of gold,' he said. That made Solomon's eyes light up.

'Is she old?'

'No, your majesty, she would be about twenty-five summers.' The envoy once again saw the King's eyes light-up, and then a frown.

'Is she ugly?'

'On the contrary my lord, by many she is thought to be one of the most beautiful women in creation'. Akil could almost feel the reward he would receive jingling in his pocket. The King had a thought, and the frown reappeared.

'Is there a King of Sheba?'

'No my lord,' said Akil, thinking 'This is going to be my most successful trip.'

As he left the palace Akil was in a state of delirious euphoria; the reward had been well beyond his wildest expectations. 'I'm a rich man,' he thought. He was, but there was to be a price to pay.

The next day he received a summons to attend the King. No sooner was he in the King's presence than he was told to proceed immediately to Sheba and take a 'Royal Invitation' for the Queen to visit King Solomon in Jerusalem.

'And if you fail, you will be no friend of mine,' added the King.

The veiled threat was not lost on the envoy. The euphoria of the previous day was seriously dampened as he left the palace to make the preparations for the journey south again. He had been home for just two days. Before going to the market to arrange a small caravan for the journey he carefully hid most of the reward inside his house. Together with a retinue of half-a-dozen men, he left just before dawn the next day.

On the journey south, which took just under three moons, Akil spent much of the time pondering on how he would manage to ensure that the Queen of Sheba accepted King Solomon's invitation. Eventually he decided that he would adopt two approaches. The first would be to tell the Queen that King Solomon, because of his renowned wisdom, would be able to answer any question that she might wish to ask him, no matter how difficult. Akil was fairly confident that Solomon's fame would have travelled as far as Sheba. The next approach would be to stress that in Jerusalem, with the help of King Solomon, a means of trading the produce of Sheba with the rest of the world could be established, and this would be of great advantage to Sheba.

Afterwards, Akil could only guess which of his arguments had held sway. But the Queen had accepted the invitation and he travelled back to Jerusalem with a much lighter heart than on his outward journey.

✦

It was only a tiny noise – virtually inaudible. But it was the wrong noise, at the wrong time, in the wrong place, and Kariz was instantly awake. He had been part of the Queen of Sheba's retinue for eleven summers and had risen to be the chief bodyguard by virtue *of his extreme loyalty, heightened sensory awareness and impressive fighting skills, which over the years had become legendary.*

The caravan was only ten days out of Marib on its long journey north to Jerusalem where the Queen was to meet King Solomon. Just one moon earlier she had sent word accepting the invitation. In the tent next to the one where Kariz was sleeping was the chest that contained jewels worth a queen's ransom and which were to be a gift to King Solomon. In the treasure tent were two soldiers who had been assigned to sleep alongside the chest.

Kariz was quickly on his feet and at the entrance flap of his tent with no more noise than a shadow flitting across the sand. First he looked towards the Queen's tent: the two bodyguards outside were standing up and not squatting down, so they had heard the noise. Of course they would not leave their posts. A glance at the 'treasure tent' a few paces away to the right showed that all was not well. Its entrance flap was not secured as he had set it earlier.

One of the many camels which were bedded-down to the left of the camp grunted in its sleep, and then there was another noise, from within the treasure tent – a muffled gurgling gasping sound, just like the one that had awakened him. Within the space of two heartbeats, and with less noise than a single heartbeat, he was inside the tent.

Many believed that Kariz could see in the dark, and that was not far from the truth. What he saw were the bodies of two dead soldiers with their throats cut. He also saw, in the near total darkness, the outline of two people who should not have been there – the assassins. Neither of these intruders was aware of anyone else within the confines of the tent before it was far too late for them to make their peace with their maker. Neither of them saw or heard the avenger of evil that despatched them from this life.

As soon as Kariz was sure that there were no more intruders in the immediate area and that the Queen's tent was safe, he went to where the rest of the bodyguards were sleeping and quietly awoke four of them. Two were sent to stand guard outside the treasure tent while Kariz and the other two made their way in a well-practised manner, silently and stealthily, unseen and unheard through the camp, then a hundred paces north from the edge of the camped caravan. Kariz then indicated to them that they should circle to the right while he set off to circle the camp in the opposite direction.

When the two bodyguards were almost due east of the camp they came across two brigands hiding among some rocks with four tethered camels. These two were much younger, neither of them had seen fifteen summers, and neither of them saw another dawn. They were barely aware that they had been discovered and had not even drawn their daggers before they were despatched.

'Is this all of them?' whispered Kariz.

'Yes, leader. We've checked the area within hundred paces.'

Satisfied that there were no more brigands in the area, they returned to the camp. Kariz told them that they could return to their tent. Although the bodyguards were far too fired-up to sleep, that was not the case with Kariz. After he had arranged for the removal of the bodies of the two murdered soldiers he went to his own tent and was asleep within the time taken by twenty heartbeats, or more accurately he fell into a state of suspended animation from which he could emerge in an instant.

The sky was just becoming light enough to draw the outline of the distant mountains. Kariz had mustered his twelve bodyguards close to the Queen's tent ready to form a protective presence around her when she made her usual appearance before her subjects at dawn. The bodies of the two dead soldiers had been wrapped in cloths and laid with their heads pointing towards where the Sun God would make his appearance. Ordek, commander of the soldiers – now reduced to fifty-eight – who were accompanying the caravan, stood ten paces further from the royal tent, slightly to the left of Kariz, with the soldiers arranged in four ranks. The remaining fifty or so people who made up the rest of the caravan were assembled in front of the soldiers.

One of the Queen's attendants rattled a tambourine, everyone became silent, and as the Queen came out from her tent, the whole assembly turned to face her, knelt and bowed their heads. The tambourine was slapped. This was the signal for all to stand and face to the East. Then at the first glimpse of the dazzling orb as it burst through the distant horizon the tambourine was slapped for a second time and everyone fell prostrate before its presence, and remained there until the orb in all its majesty was visible, which was signalled by a third slap of the tambourine. The spirits of the dead soldiers were offered to the Sun God and then their bodies were placed on a funeral pyre, which had been prepared earlier by their former comrades. The bodies of the brigands, including the two outside the camp's perimeter, were gathered up and thrown among the rocks for the wild animals and carrion to dispose of.

Once the funeral pyre had burnt down, the long hard journey to Jerusalem was resumed. It was to take a further one hundred dusty thirsty days, much of it across a barren waterless land, until they reached the fertile crescent in the land of milk and honey.

The attempted robbery was only the start of their problems.

Ordek, who had been selected for this journey to Jerusalem, had been part of the Queen's retinue for twelve summers. He had been in the employ of her majesty for just over a year before Kariz appeared on the scene.

'Why should he be chosen over me to lead the royal bodyguard and be closer to the Queen?' He had asked this question of all those who had joined the royal household over the past ten years, ever since Kariz had been elevated to his present high position within the court. 'It doesn't seem fair' was the invariable reply. Not because that is what they thought – they were all aware of the reasons Kariz held the position that he did. Those who were asked indulged Ordek and agreed with him because he was known to have a fiery temper and a vicious and malicious streak. They all knew that he could and would make life very unpleasant for them if they showed any kind of support for Kariz.

Kariz was quite puzzled as to how the two brigands had managed to get into the encampment undetected by Ordek's perimeter guards. 'They wouldn't have got past any of my men,' *he thought. During the brief skirmish he had immediately assessed – as a matter of instinct – that the intruders were not very competent and should not have got past any sentries. When he mentioned his concern to Ordek the only reply that he received was:*

'Are you trying to blame me, so that you don't look so bad in the eyes of the Queen? And why did you wait until sunrise to let me know that two of my men had been killed while they were guarding the treasure? I expect you were just trying to make yourself look good. Don't think that I haven't noticed the way she looks at you.'

Kariz didn't pursue the matter, not because he was afraid of Ordek. He stood a head and shoulders above the commander and had a physique that was a testament to his years of unrelenting training, but he knew from past experience that it would serve no good purpose.

CHAPTER THREE

David told Jack that he was supposed to go to stay with a distant aunt at Gravesend. Fortunately the arrangement was only tentative. David's father – apparently he was a schoolmaster – seemed to have very little idea of the distances in London, and he'd obviously not heard of any of the tales that Jack thought were common knowledge; lurid stories that were boastfully circulated among the seafaring community, and which related to the temptations that could confront unsuspecting young men who ventured into Gravesend. *'I don't think he's quite ready for that,'* thought Jack, remembering guiltily a certain skipper's sister back in Grimsby. Following Jack's suggestion the two of them went to the Salvation Army canteen, where they were able to get tea and sandwiches, 'char and 'wad' becoming two new words for David's vocabulary. Also they obtained an address where they could get cheap clean accommodation, safe from any temptation, for a couple of nights.

'Bloody hell, Dave! You didn't tell me it was for 22 years. I'd be an old man by the time I got out,' said Jack, completely astounded by what the recruiting Sergeant had just said.

'Well, Jack, it's up to you but I know what I am going to do – I am definitely going to enlist.' David had evidently spent a lot of time thinking about it and had made this decision much earlier, although he admitted to Jack that the reality was that his father had made the decision and David had accepted it. As for Jack, he had been considering the prospect of joining the RAF for only the past 48 hours – he really needed more time. He liked to think things through more carefully before making any decision. Now he was beginning to seriously question the whole idea of coming to London.

'Hell's bells! 22 years!' But what were the alternatives? Working the trawlers was out, definitely not the steel-works, and not the mines. His thoughts went back to the row with his father, where they'd come close to blows ....

'The trouble wi' thee lad,' his father had said, 'is that tha don't realise what struggle 'tis t' keep t' family off t' parish.'

'Oh yes I do – don't I send money home regular?'

'Aye and what's tha going to do now? Nowt?'

'I've helped a lot. I've done my bit and I'll keep on helping thee, but I've got a life to live and I want more than this.' He recalled how he'd swept his arm in a gesture of contempt around the shabby room, furnished with the best that poverty could buy.

That had hurt his father. Had he meant to be so cruel to the Old Man?

'Well, mister high and bloody mighty, if that's the way tha feels, tha can bloody well bugger off again and well manage wi'out thee and tha money.'

David was speaking and suddenly Jack was back in the present.

'I said, what are you going to do then, Jack?'

It was decision time. What was he going to do? Big decision time, crucial life-changing decision time ... a deep breath.

'OK, Dave. I'm with you.'

David's face lit up. It was as if the past two days in Jack's company had been just about the best in his life. Jack wondered if David had many friends – or any friends at all. Perhaps he'd just been under the thumb of his parents all his life.

'Oh that's great, Jack. I'm sure you won't regret it.'

'Hold on, you two. Let's not get carried away,' interrupted the Recruiting Sergeant. 'Nowadays the Royal Air Force wants people to train for useful trades ...'

'I know. My father ...'

The look from the Sergeant made David wish that he'd kept quiet.

'It's not that easy,' continued the Sergeant. 'You will have to take tests and even if you pass them you will have to get through a medical examination at the training camp.'

This was more news for Jack. Even though David must have known about the tests, he'd presumably decided to keep quiet about them in case they might have put Jack off. David waited until he was certain that the Sergeant was not going to say anything else.

'Nothing to worry about, Jack – it's straightforward enough,' he said cheerfully. 'My father told me that it is only basic Arithmetic and English with a few observation tests.' He did not tell Jack that he had failed his Matriculation and that his bitterly disappointed parents could hardly live with the shame of it.

'That's OK for you, Dave, but you're forgetting that I only went to the Elementary School.'

What Jack didn't tell him that he'd been the star pupil, and that his schoolmaster had pleaded with his father to let him go on to the Technical School.

His father had been dead against it, of course: 'I tell thee summat, schoolmaster – by the time I was young Jack's age I'd been in t' steel-works for nearly two years. I don't 'old wi' all this fancy education. 'E can read and write well enough, and come t' Christmas 'e can start there t' 'elp support family. So I'd be obliged t' thee t' stop putting fancy ideas in t' young lad's 'ead.'

The Old Man had made a decision and that was that. The schoolmaster had realised that there was no point in arguing against it and had reluctantly given up trying.

'There's no need to look at me like that, mother,' his Old Man had said. 'Tha knows times are 'ard and young Jack can 'elp quite a bit. Tha knows what struggle 'tis t' keep off t' Parish, and tha knows what I think about charity.'

Jack had been bitterly disappointed but had said nothing, and his face had given no clue to his feelings.

Several days after the schoolmaster's visit, the family had

been in the scullery – mother, Jack, Cissy – who was the next eldest after Jack – younger brother Alan, and Doris the baby. The hooter that signalled the end of work for the day had sounded at its normal time but the Old Man had come in a little earlier than usual. He'd looked worn-out.

'Where's tea then, missus? Should be ont' table.'

All of the pent-up disappointment and frustration within Jack had suddenly exploded.

'Tha's just not fair to me mother – tha treats 'er like a bloody skivvy, thee old bugger,' he had blurted out.

In all of our lives there are words that we wish we had not uttered and so it had been with Jack on that occasion. It wasn't the stinging blow around the head that had sent him reeling across the scullery and nearly into the shiny blackened cooking range, that had made Jack regret the outburst – it was because what he had said was not true. Although he'd felt sorry for himself, Jack had also felt rather ashamed. He had been well aware that his father was devoted to his mother. The Old Man was no hard-drinking wife beater, as was all too common in the area. No-one had worked harder to try to make life easier for his wife than Jack Toulson senior. He even went grave-digging before starting work at six o'clock in order to bring in a little extra money.

'Tha'll not swear at thee father, or I'll thrash thee wi' in an inch of tha life.'

Jack couldn't recall ever having seen his father this angry before. He had known it was not the swearing that had upset the Old Man so much. Jack had sworn at his father before, although blasphemous language had earned him a taste of the belt on one occasion. Jack had begun to feel more ashamed as he'd recalled the time, the winter before, when his father had been off work with an injury for two weeks and there'd been no money coming from the steel-works. His mother had nearly collapsed when she came in from a scrubbing job that she'd taken over Ilkley way, despite the fact she was ill. The Old Man, despite his injury, had managed to get her into bed with Jack's help. Later that night he'd seen the Old Man, the 'hard man' of the steel-works, kneeling and crying at his wife's bedside. He would never know that Jack had seen him.

Oh yes, Jack had regretted his outburst, but what is said can't be un-said. The Old Man may have been hurt by Jack's words, but he would have despised Jack if he had apologised and Jack knew that. 'A man must stand by what he says and does' was the code by which his father lived and Jack was cast in the same mould.

About a week later, when the family had been having their evening meal, Jack had turned to his father and asked: 'Can I give thee 'and wi' graves tomorrow?'

His father had looked at him, their eyes locked on one another in a long unspoken conversation.

'Aye, tha can that, lad. T' would be a reet 'elp.'

※

The tests were not quite as simple as David had said, and despite his reassuring comments beforehand, David only just scraped through, whereas Jack passed with flying colours. Although David was pleased for Jack he was perhaps a little jealous and visibly disappointed with his own performance.

'Reckon I was just lucky, Dave,' said Jack, trying to make his new friend feel less inadequate. But he did wonder how different his life might have been if his Old Man had let him go to the Technical School.

※

Four days later, as the train stuttered to a hissing halt, the off-white letters on the faded green boards spaced along the tiny platform informed the train's occupants that this was Dumpton Park. Jack recalled how apt the name Grimesthorpe was for his home in Sheffield. He wondered if this place was equally well named. It certainly didn't look very exciting.

'This is where we get off, Jack,' said David, already on his feet and taking his case down from the rack – Jack didn't need telling. They'd already carefully studied their travel documents and the destination was clearly stated on them.

'Calm down, Dave – the train won't leave straight away.'

'Well you must admit, Jack, it is rather exciting,' said

David, keen to see what the day had in store.

'Right you are then – let's go and see what we're letting ourselves in for,' said Jack, not wanting to dampen his friend's enthusiasm. Truth to be told, a little of David's enthusiasm was beginning to rub-off on Jack, despite the fact that he was still in the throes of coming to terms with the thought of a twenty-two year commitment.

As they disembarked and collected their belonging together, they could see along the platform other small uncertain groups similarly occupied with their luggage. In all there were about three dozen young men; no-one was quite sure what to do next. A copper-haired young man who was standing a few yards away from Jack and David picked up his belongings and approached the duo rather like a stray seeking the security of the herd.

'Hello, off to join the RAF as well?' he enquired with an affected air of nonchalance.

'We certainly are,' replied David with quite a show of eagerness.

'I'm Ted Sawyer,' said the newcomer, quickly adding 'but I expect that you've already guessed that everyone calls me Ginger.'

'Nice to meet you, Ginger,' chipped in Jack, signalling acceptance of the nickname. 'This is Dave White and I'm Jack Toulson.'

'I suppose they call you Chalky,' said Ginger nodding towards David, who began to look a little ill at ease. He didn't look like the sort of person to ever have had a nickname before: Jack had noticed his slight hesitation in replying when he had first addressed him as 'Dave'.

But, bowing to the inevitable, and presumably anxious to obtain acceptance in his new life, David replied: 'Chalky is OK by me.'

'You two fancy a Woodbine?' Ginger asked, taking a crumpled packet of five from the breast pocket of his jacket. 'These paper packs are worse than bloody useless,' he muttered by way of apologising for the somewhat less than pristine condition of the cigarettes he was offering round. They both took one and lit up. Jack smiled when David coughed a little, then tried to cover it up – smoking was another new experience, he guessed. Nevertheless he made a passably good job of it.

They'd taken but a few puffs when onto the platform strode an RAF NCO. The precision of his stride, manner of his bearing and general turnout were quite striking. The hazy sunlight reflected from his polished cap-badge and the toes of his boots added to the overall crispness of his appearance. Although he was only of medium height, his erect posture made him seem taller. He was a bullish man with strong hard features, which created neither a paternal or avuncular impression. The only concession to age was a slight greying of the hair at the temples, which otherwise was strikingly black just like David's. The clicking of the studded boots on the concrete and cobbles had produced an expectant silence. Before he'd uttered a word, Sergeant Major King had commanded the attention of the would-be airmen.

'Good morning, gentlemen – I assume that you are all for RAF Manston?'

There was an uncoordinated sound of agreement from the assembly on the platform. David, newly christened 'Chalky', quickly removed his cigarette although Jack and Ginger didn't bother.

'If you would all assemble outside the station, we've got some trucks waiting that will take you to the air-base. Oh, and no smoking in the lorries, if you don't mind, gentlemen.'

Jack and Ginger stubbed out their cigarettes. Bags, cases and brown paper parcels were gathered up and the young men followed the Sergeant Major out of the station, no-one wanting to be first – not even Chalky – and certainly no-one wanted to be last.

There were two canvas-covered trucks waiting in the road and soon everyone was milling around them.

'Get aboard, then!' the Sergeant Major shouted.

Hesitantly at first, some of those nearest one of the trucks started to clamber aboard, then others began to throw their luggage to those already embarked and quickly scramble into the truck themselves.

'Come on, then – don't all try to get in the one truck. There are two of them,' King yelled.

The herding of the young men into the cramped confines of the two lorries seemed to act as the catalyst that broke down the barriers of reserve that had been so apparent on the platform.

'Same every bleeding time – no sooner do they get into the transport than they start twittering like a flock of effing sparrows,' said the Corporal in the second lorry to the driver sitting next to him. The driver nodded agreement.

'You're right there, Corp – they'll learn. Don't think we've left any behind, so let's go. Don't want to keep ol' King waiting.'

The journey was quite short and although rather uncomfortable everyone was so engrossed in conversation that they hardly noticed it. In what seemed like no time at all they'd arrived. Following the command of 'everybody out' barked out by the Sergeant Major there was a general anxious bustling searching for luggage followed by an enthusiastic clambering to get out of the transport.

'Can't one of you morons let down those tail-gates?' bawled King.

In an attempt to obey, an anxious occupant of the first lorry pulled out the two retaining pins, and without warning, the tailgate flew open. In the process one of those who had already disembarked was hit on the head and knocked unconscious. Two others fell out of the lorry – one hurt his arm, the other his ankle.

'Bleeding hell!' exclaimed the Corporal. 'It's just like something out of the Keystone Cops.'

No-one asked who'd pulled the pins out, but one look at David's face told Jack who'd been responsible. He edged over to him and said in a very quiet voice:

'There's no need to say anything.'

'But Jack ...'

Jack shook his head slightly and David kept quiet.

The Corporal alongside the driver of the first lorry double marched to the sickbay to get help while the rest of the group was ushered into one of the 'buildings'.

'No, this is not a ruddy dormitory.' These were the words of the Corporal that met them as they entered the building. 'This will be your Flight.'

He went on to describe how the squadron was made up

of three flights. This group was to be Flight C. To make it clear he repeated the quarters were also known as Flights. Some still appeared to be confused after the explanation.

'Now find yourselves a bed, and dump your bags on it, then we'll go over to the Stores and get you lot kitted out, and then it'll be time for the medical.' Something seemed to amuse him when he said this. He didn't pause for them to take it all in, but went straight on. 'On the command "get fell-in outside" I want you all to go out on to the road there,' he said, pointing to where they'd just been, 'and line up in three rows facing your Flight.'

That confused a few.

'Fall-in outside!' shouted the Corporal. Everybody hurried to comply.

At the Quartermaster's stores the issuing Sergeant explained to them how lucky they were to be getting these new uniforms. He said it as if he personally was responsible for paying for all the kit they were to be issued with.

'Some of us remember, not long ago, when we had to make do with a mixture of old army and navy uniforms,' he said. 'In fact we looked a bit like Fred Karno's Army. But now because Air Marshal Trenchard intends to have a very smart RAF, you lot are going to be properly turned-out. All of you make sure that you look after it. Woe betide anyone who loses anything.'

With that, the issue went ahead from best-blues to 'drawers, cellular, airmen for the use of'. The recruits struggled with carrying their new uniforms back to the Flight where they dumped their acquisitions onto their beds. However before they had time to try on the uniforms it was time for the medical inspection. They were told once again to 'fall in' outside and were marched off to the sickbay and ushered into a large hall. They had been told that when the Medical Officer reached them they were to drop their trousers and stand with their hands above their head. Although Jack was no stranger to the sight of naked bodies, or of being naked in front of others – bath-night at home at home had been the tin bath in front of the stove – he felt as much ill at ease as the others. As for David, whose nickname of Chalky just hadn't stuck, he appeared to be suffering agonies of anticipated embarrassment.

His face was a brilliant crimson. The young men stood in two rows, one on either side of the room, facing inwards and facing each other, stripped to the waist waiting for the MO. The real embarrassment occurred when the doctor, squatting to navel level, lifted the recruit's penis with a pencil and peered inquisitively at it and the surrounding area using a torch to aid him in his genitalia exploration. Only one of those in the Flight shamed himself. When the pencil was deployed his penis started to lift of its own accord. This was soon corrected by the MO with a sharp flick of the pencil. This brought the offending member into line and tears to the eyes of the unfortunate recruit. In the future the 'freedom from infection inspections' – the dreaded FFIs – were to become an altogether routine occurrence.

After this, each recruit in turn went into a series of rooms situated at the end of the hall for various examinations including hearing, eyesight, having their scrota clutched and being told to cough as well as other checks. The Medical, including the jabs, lasted just over an hour. Four of the group failed and were sent off to return their kit and pick up railway warrants, to get back home.

'They've got it arse-about-face!' exclaimed Jack. 'Why didn't they do the Medical first?'

'What are you complaining about, Jack?' said David, who was clearly relieved that the ordeal was now over. The colour in his cheeks was beginning to subside. 'You, me and Ginger came through all right.'

'Nearly didn't though,' retorted Jack. 'I came close to thumping that medic when he squeezed my balls.'

They all laughed including David and it seemed to relieve the tension that had been gradually building up since their arrival.

After they'd all signed on the dotted line and sworn allegiance to His Majesty the King, it was lunch in the Airmen's Mess. At least the food was quite good.

'Well that's it then – twenty-two years,' thought Jack.

After lunch they were marched – if you could call it that – back to their Flight where they were to renew their acquaintance with Sergeant Major King. He now seemed to be a very different person to the one that had met them at the station. There was no longer any pretence of friendliness in his face. Wearing their new uniforms, many of which – despite the quartermaster's eloquent praise of what they had been issued with – were ill-fitting, the recruits were all lined up standing alongside the beds that they'd chosen. The Corporal brought them to attention before King began. He started to pace up and down the Flight with a slow, measured, deliberate step. The expression on his face made all the recruits feel very apprehensive and they were soon to discover that their fears were not misplaced.

'Some of you may have ideas of eventually becoming officers so that you can lord it over us humble NCOs who have worked very hard to get where we are,' said King. 'Well let me tell you it's not going to be that easy – if you wanted it easy you should have gone to the college at Cranwell. Of course, for that you would need to be educated.' He paused. 'Do any of you bright sparks have one of these fancy new education certificates?'

Briefly he seemed lost in his own thoughts – he was, and it was always the same. It was back to the summer of 1900, back to the time when he was stationed in the garrison at Catterick. It had been the most wonderful but most tragic time of his life. He'd joined the Army at the age of 14 as a boy soldier; five years later he'd risen to the rank of lance corporal. One Sunday afternoon he had been walking in the nearby village of Richmond when he'd caught sight of a young lady walking with what he had taken to be her mother, who had been dressed in the fashion of the queen – all in black complete with cape and bustle. The young lady, by way of contrast, had been dressed all in white with a broad-brimmed lacy hat. He had become immediately besotted. For the next four Sundays he'd made a point of being in the village at the same time, and on three of those occasions he had caught sight of her again. The Sunday after that not only had he caught sight of her, he'd actually caught her eye. She had smiled demurely but the mother had seen this and hastily pulled her away. That would have been the end of it, but luck was to shine on him before the cup of happiness was to be snatched from his lips. This time it had been a Saturday afternoon two weeks later when he'd been walking along the footpath on the bank of the small river just outside the village. He had walked past a woman asleep on a picnic rug a few feet from the path. He had immediately recognised her as the young lady's mother. He had walked only about a dozen paces when he'd come face to face with the young lady herself. They had smiled at each other, and she had nodded her head in the direction of the sleeping mother. She'd leaned across and whispered in his ear, and a tryst had been arranged, one of half a dozen that were to take place over the next two months. She'd never told him her name so he'd called her 'petal', as she had reminded him of the softness of a flower with a complexion to match a soft pink rose. He had known her name was Betty, though, because he had seen it embroidered on her handkerchief.

Then one day disaster had struck. They had been in the process of parting at the end of what turned out to be the last of their meetings. She had still been touching his hand as they walked on the path towards the village when, by an unfortunate coincidence, her father – out walking with his dog in a nearby lane – had seen them. He had immediately hurried across the rough ground between the lane and the path to confront them. All the time he had been shouting 'Get away from him, young lady – get away from him'. The fact that he'd stumbled into a patch of stinging nettles on the way hadn't helped. Purple in the face with anger and shaking his walking stick he had turned to the soldier and bellowed: 'I forbid you, a common soldier, to associate with my daughter. You are not to contact her in any way. She is not for the likes of you, or any of your "sort". She is of gentry stock, and I will decide with whom she keeps chaperoned company. Let me assure you they will be well educated and proper young gentlemen, certainly none of your ilk. Now be off with you before I send for the constable! Come along now, my dear! Your mother and I will have words with you when we get home.' With that, he had quite forcefully grabbed her by the arm and led her away.

After his humiliating experience at the hands of Betty's father he'd returned to the garrison to lick his wounds. Her father had written to the garrison commander, and when he had been hauled-up in front of the commanding Officer, King had discovered that Betty's father and his superior had gone to the same public school, one for the education of 'the sons of upper-class families'. The CO had made a point of stressing this, rubbing salt into King's wound. He had also made it clear that King had come within a whisker of losing his hard-earned stripe. Entered into his record had been the words: 'he has an inability to conduct himself correctly in the presence of superior young women'. This made it even more difficult for him to gain further promotion.

How Henry King detested educated young men! And how that resentment had festered and fed upon itself, to become a downright bitter hatred over the years.

Six months later, after being part of a special guard of honour at Queen Victoria's funeral, he had been redeployed to Aldershot, never again to see Betty. By the time of the outbreak of the Great War, despite what had been entered on his record at Catterick, he'd risen to the rank of Sergeant, met and married – but never loved – Eunice, who was ten years his junior. When the RFC was deployed to France in 1914 King had been at first seconded to it and then permanently attached, and had been promoted to Sergeant Major just before the RFC became the RAF. But he had never lost his utter contempt and hatred of 'the educated class' as he called them.

He abruptly returned from his self-pitying ruminations as David and one other member of the Flight cautiously half-raised their hands in slow motion in answer to the apparently harmless question. King stopped his pacing.

'No, you dozy pair, in the Royal Air Force we don't put up our hands,' he bawled. 'What do you think this is? A school? No, you misbegotten lot, you come smartly to attention, or if you are already at attention, you take a short step forward'. Click! Slam! 'Like that,' said King, having taken one pace forward with a practised precision acquired over many years. 'Well until our two young gentlemen here have become officers, and while you are all on this camp learning how to be common airmen, there are a few things that I would like you to understand very clearly.' There was a progressive iciness creeping into his voice, like water freezing across the surface of a pond.

'Although I am not the King that you that you've sworn allegiance to, it might just as well have been ...' There was a long pause, a very long pause. Then, with the suddenness of an animal pouncing, he snapped in a voice that could have been easily heard outside: 'You do what I say, when I say, in the way that I say, without question or delay. No matter how well educated you are!' He spun on his heels and glowered menacingly at David.

'Ye –e –es, Sergeant Major' stuttered David so nervously that it made quite a few of the other members of the Flight equally ill at ease, especially the other recruit who'd half put up his hand.

Since leaving school at the age of twelve, Jack had come up against quite a few bullies and would-be bullies, and he'd always managed to handle them. He recognised another one in the form of King. *'It won't work with me,'* thought Jack.

Turning abruptly to Jack, the Sergeant Major demanded 'what about you, lad?'

It was almost as if he'd been listening to Jack's thoughts.

'I understand,' said Jack, thinking *'you bullying bastard'* to complete his reply.

'I understand ... Sergeant Major,' snarled the NCO, slowly enunciating the words 'Sergeant Major'.

'I understand, Sergeant Major,' repeated Jack, keeping his unflinching gaze directly to the front.

After King had finished his 'talk' to the new recruits and left, they found themselves in the charge of Corporal Rydal, who seemed downright friendly in comparison, despite the fact that he spent the next quarter of an hour telling them what they could and couldn't do – and what they would do, or else! The difference between him and King was that he appeared to have the humanity that seemed to be totally lacking in the Sergeant Major.

Reading between the lines of what Corporal Rydal said to them, they realised they would have to be extremely careful not to get on the wrong side of the Sergeant Major. Jack noticed that, for some reason, when the Corporal was giving this warning he was looking directly at David and the other recruit who had put his hand up.

Before 'lights out' that night they were joined by the three who'd been involved in the accident in getting out of the truck.

Fortunately for them they'd missed the first onslaught of the Sergeant Major's tongue. Unfortunately for them, they hadn't heard the Corporal's warnings.

David, Ginger and Jack had picked three beds alongside one another – the selection had been mostly David's doing; the other two didn't wish to upset him and had fallen in with what he'd arranged. By now even Ginger had abandoned the attempt to nickname David as Chalky – it just didn't seem to fit.

'You know what?' said David, just before lights out. 'If we three stick together, we are going to be alright.'

'Yes, but it's going to be tricky protecting you from that bastard King,' was Jack's unspoken reply. *Protecting him?* It occurred to Jack that he was already looking on David as a younger brother. What the heck he thought – somebody's got to look out for him.

CHAPTER FOUR

It was towards the middle of the day when one of the bodyguards from the second watch brought his camel alongside that of Kariz. After the customary greeting the bodyguard reported that he had seen a fleeting glimpse of something glinting near the base of the hills just to the west of the route that they were taking, and halfway to the horizon. This was the sort of alertness that Kariz had instilled in all his men.

At the end of the day when the caravan had encamped, and as soon as the evening meal had been eaten – the bodyguards always ate their meals together sitting near the Queen's tent and separate from the rest of the entourage – Kariz held a meeting to let his men know of a plan that he had devised.

'I need two volunteers to carry out a clandestine reconnoitre exercise,' he said. 'It will mean losing a night's sleep.'

As usual there was no shortage of volunteers: the whole group, to a man, wanted to go. Kariz selected the two that he considered the best for the task, one of whom was the youngest of the bodyguards and had been part of the 'elite band' for only two years. They were instructed to leave the camp unobserved and, under the cover of darkness, to proceed to the area where the suspicious flash of light had been seen, which by now was about ten thousand paces away.

Because it was the night after the new moon, it was very dark.

As soon as the two volunteers were satisfied that all of members of the caravan were asleep, except for Ordek's soldiers and the Queen's duty bodyguards, they un-tethered their camels from where they had been bedded down with the rest of the herd and silently led them, unseen by the perimeter sentries, out of the camp and off in a north-westerly direction. They returned two hours before dawn to report back to Kariz, who then awoke and assembled most of the 'elite band'. The more senior of the two bodyguards, in a hushed voice, gave details of what had happened on their expedition.

'We travelled until we reached the base of the range of hills to the west when we heard a number of people talking,' he said. 'We thought they could be associates of the devils that broke into the treasure tent and killed those two soldiers. We tethered our camels eight hundred paces from their encampment, taking care not to break the skyline, then circled the target. I went on the right circle and Asaph went on the left, and, much to our surprise, we discovered there were no posted sentries. It seemed very strange but the whole group was awake. We approached as close as possible.'

Kariz knew that this would have been less than ten paces.

'Could you hear what they were saying?' he asked.

'Yes. They were all talking about what they would do when they became rich. The conversations kept overlapping and it was hard to follow at times, but they were clearly worried about what had happened to their four missing men. None of them seemed to have any idea as to why the men hadn't returned.'

'How large a group were they?'

'There were ten of them. Two spoke in a tongue that we didn't understand. We gathered that they intend to sleep all of tomorrow, remain hidden and let our caravan pass, then follow us until the next new moon. Then, when the moon is halfway to the horizon, they plan to sneak into the camp.'

'I'd like to see them try!' said Kariz. 'They failed last time and they will fail again.'

The bodyguard making the report started to say something, then closed his mouth.

'What?' said Kariz. 'Speak up, man.'

'It was their leader, sir. What he said ... I remember his words exactly. It was about Ordek.'

'Ordek?' Kariz jumped to his feet. 'Tell me.'

'He said "don't forget that on the nights of the new moon, my brother Ordek will arrange that the sentries on the south perimeter will be the five soldiers that are with us."'

There was a gasp of surprise from the bodyguards. 'His brother? So that's how they did it before!' exclaimed one of the men.

'Apparently Ordek's brother sent two men to find out how the treasure chest was guarded. They accidently disturbed the guards, panicked and killed them. That aroused the Royal bodyguards who killed the two brigands and then killed their nephews who were guarding the camels. Although they still don't seem to have enough information about the guarding of the treasure tent, they plan to carry out their raid at the next new moon. Apparently, Ordek sometimes leaves messages behind when the caravan sets out in the mornings.'

'Is that everything you heard?' asked Kariz.

'Well, the men seemed unhappy about not being told earlier about the four that had died. One of them was muttering "He's known about it all day, I'm not sure that we can trust him." Then they returned to talking about how they would spend the fortunes that they would be coming into. At that point, we just quietly slipped away'.

As a result of the report, Kariz instructed two of his men to watch Ordek each morning before the caravan set out on the next stage of its journey, to see if he was leaving messages for his brother.

The time until the next new moon seemed to pass very slowly indeed. It was a very tense and difficult period knowing that there were six traitors within the caravan but not knowing who five of them were. When the caravan set off on the morning before the next new moon, those who were secretly watching Ordek reported that he had fallen behind and had caught up a short time later.

Towards the end of that day Kariz approached the senior advisor to request an audience with the Queen; it was promptly granted. During the audience he informed the Queen of what had been discovered and of a strategy that he had devised.

After the meal that evening, Kariz met with Ordek and told him that he had the Queen's permission to take six of his bodyguards to 'scout out' the land ahead because evidence of recent tracks had been seen during the day.

'I'm sorry if this makes extra work for you and your men,

Ordek,' he said, *'but the Queen thinks that this might be a wise precaution.'*

Ordek had been on the point of objecting, but he paused. Kariz, who was very good at reading faces, saw the momentary smirk on Ordek's face when he grudgingly accepted what Kariz was going to do.

'I suppose you have to keep in the Queen's favour,' he said, while thinking 'You won't find anything ahead, and you're playing right into my hands.'

As soon as Kariz disappeared into the darkness with his group, going in a northerly direction, Ordek couldn't control the smile on his face. One of his sentries on the northern perimeter, who was just going on duty, was quite unsettled when Ordek exchanged pleasantries with him. The smile on Ordek's face would have soon disappeared if he had known that once the scouting group were a thousand paces from the camp they turned east and then circled round until they were two thousand paces south-east of the encampment, where they bedded down their camels since they knew that the attack would be coming from the south-west. One of the bodyguards stayed with the camels, the other five followed Kariz and moved closer to the camp, spreading out in a line parallel to the camp perimeter, about a thousand paces from it, with two hundred paces between each of the bodyguards. They then settled down and melded into the terrain in a way that they had practised many times, to wait. It would have been possible to pass within touching distance of any of them and not be aware of their presence.

The would-be robbers passed to the east of the first of the bodyguards but the camel of one of the brigands walked directly over the second bodyguard at the western end of the line. The line had been a protective procedure, to make sure that they heard the intruders, but as it turned out, the intruders were not practised in furtive manoeuvres and although they thought that they were being very quiet, everyone in the line heard them – they were far from stealthy by Kariz's standards. Five hundred paces from the caravan the brigands tethered their camels, but didn't leave anyone guarding them. They then all proceeded to approach the camp on foot. As they reached the perimeter, six shadowy figures joined them. This was the prearranged trigger for the bodyguards. The one on the extreme western end of the line detached himself from his lair.

It was almost as if part of the surroundings had metamorphosed to become a man – he moved to the next position where he was joined by that bodyguard, who despite the pain from the gash in his thigh – the result of being trodden on by the camel – followed his comrade to the next position. The process was repeated until all of the 'line' was gathered near the camels.

At the same time one of the six men that Kariz had left behind in the camp, the one supposedly guarding the treasure but who, in reality, had been watching the sentries on the southern perimeter from a hiding place, slipped silently between the tents from his position, as soon as he saw Ordek and the five treacherous sentries join forces with the bandits. He went to collect three of his colleagues, first the two who were in the treasure tent and then young Asaph, who was in the Queen's tent. As they had been instructed to do, the four of them made their way to the north side of one of the tents in the south-east corner of the camp, melded into the surroundings and waited.

With their accomplices, Ordek and his brother made their way to the treasure tent.

'No need to worry about that "full of himself" Kariz interfering this time,' muttered Ordek. 'He's so clever that he's gone off to the north with most of his men – chasing shadows. He's left two with the treasure, and four guarding the Queen in her tent.'

They then carefully and quietly – by their standards – entered the treasure tent ready to kill those guarding the treasure. There was just enough light for them to make out the treasure chest, but there was no sign of any bodyguards.

Ordek laughed. 'They probably abandoned their posts because their high and mighty leader is not here. If it had been my men, as it should have been, they wouldn't have dared leave their posts. I wouldn't be surprised if they are over at the women's tents.'

They briefly considered taking the Queen with them as hostage, but decided against that idea – they would stick with the original plan to carry out a clandestine robbery.

Nevertheless, they had an uneasy feeling that something was wrong, so they quickly went about seizing the unguarded treasure chest and making their escape. Two of the soldier sentries-turned-bandits were ordered to carry the chest. And the whole group quietly – by their standards – set off to the southern perimeter. As the brigands made their way past the perimeter the four bodyguards in the camp, unseen and unheard by the bandits, formed a line behind them, and stealthily followed. Kariz, with his men now spread out in a line – each man three paces from the next so that they formed a barrier between the intruders and their camels – quietly, purposefully and slowly, moved towards the robbers.

The trap had slowly and quietly closed. The raiders had gone less than a hundred paces when they saw seven shadowy figures approaching. The men carrying the chest put it down and drew their swords.

'Right, brothers, there's only seven of them,' said one, stepping forward to engage in combat.

The defecting soldiers were good, very good, but nowhere good enough for Kariz's men. Within less than fifty heartbeats, the hearts of three of the traitors and three of the brigands were no longer beating. The only bodyguard to be wounded was the one who had been injured when the camel had trodden on him. His injury had made him less agile, and as a consequence he had suffered a nasty sliced gash across his shoulders. The other two traitorous sentries decided to make a run for it back to the camp. It was then that they realised that there were not 'just seven of them'. Their cries for mercy went unheeded: the Queen's bodyguards were in no mood to be merciful. Ordek and his brother, with the remaining brigands, broke off and made a run for the camels. Kariz, with his remaining able-bodied men, jogged after the fleeing robbers and fell upon them with clinical efficiency as they tried to untie the camels' legs which Kariz's men had earlier hobbled. The last words of Ordek's brother to Ordek were 'I thought you said that you said he'd gone to ...' Ordek had no memorable last words.

The treasure chest was picked up and carried back to the treasure tent. The Queen was collected from her attendant's tent, where she had been guarded by the two bodyguards on special duty, and escorted back to her proper quarters.

Although it was less than a day since Kariz had the audience with the Queen it seemed to have been so much longer. At that audience the senior advisor who, as normal, had been present, had expressed serious reservations about parts of Kariz's plan. In addition to informing the Queen and her advisor about what had been discovered, he had explained how he intended to deploy his men to foil the intended robbery. He had suggested that after nightfall the Queen be surreptitiously moved to her attendant's tent with two bodyguards until after the raid had taken place and the culprits had been caught or despatched. Asaph would take her place in the royal tent, so that anyone who entered would assume that the Queen was still there. The Queen's advisor had not been happy with this part of the plan but Queen had been very much in favour of it and so it had been agreed that Kariz go ahead.

After the raid, when the bodyguards were sitting around talking together with others from the caravan, including some of the women, Asaph's role in the raid became the topic of conversation.

'I reckon that he dressed up in the Queen's nightclothes and lay on the bed waiting for any intruders,' said one.

'Good job no-one went in the tent. They would have been surprised by the Queen's hairy legs', replied another.

'They'd have been even more surprised to discover that she had a dick like a donkey.'

This ribald comment raised quite a few laughs. It was well known that Asaph was rather well endowed. In fact many of his colleagues were quite envious of him. Needless to say he was popular with several of the camp followers. When this story was repeated to others in the caravan it somehow became changed with the telling, and it ended up as 'the Queen has hairy legs and one foot like a goat'.

CHAPTER FIVE

At six-thirty it was already light, the sun would soon be up, reveille had been sounded and Corporal Rydal was telling those at the end of the Flight furthest from the door to get up. He then heard the familiar menacing 'click click' of the studded boots heralding the approach of Sergeant Major King. The Corporal was looking a little apprehensive and there was a general uneasy and uncertain stirring from the beds that still held occupants.

Jack had been up for almost an hour and was already washed, dressed and shaved.

'Bloody hell, Jack!' exclaimed Ginger, looking across to Jack's bed. 'Where have you been? I didn't hear you get up.'

No-one had. Over the years, Jack had developed the habit – often of necessity – of rising early, in addition to which he was a remarkably light sleeper; at the slightest sound he was awake and alert. Before Jack had a chance to reply, King stomped into the Flight with an exaggerated parade ground step. Banging the pace stick – which he appeared to carry everywhere – against the side of a tall locker near the door, he bawled 'get out of those stinking pits, you lazy bunch of namby-pambies. Anyone who hasn't got both feet on the ground on the floor in ten seconds is on a fizzer.'

Taking his cue from what he could see the Corporal doing, Jack gave David a less-than-gentle shove to get him out of bed.

David looked a little upset at Jack's apparent unkind treatment and was about to say something when events took over.

Two of the unfortunate recruits who hadn't heard the warnings about King were still in the process of easing themselves out of their beds five seconds after the stipulated time.

'Right, you two,' said King in a quiet voice that somehow held more threat than his shouting and bawling. 'You have made a very, very bad start to your lives in the Royal Air-force.' Then, in his usual aggressive loud voice, he snapped: 'Both of you report to the Flight Lieutenant's office at 1800 hours. You're both on a charge of failing to obey an order.'

'But Sergeant Major ...' one of the unfortunate pair began hesitantly.

Before he had chance to explain about his minor injury, King bellowed at him.

'Shut up! You 'orrible little airman! You don't answer me back. Ever! You speak only when I tell you or I'll 'ave you on a charge of insubordination and you'll be up before the Winco so fast that your feet won't touch the ground.'

It was as if time had stopped. Everyone in the Flight remained frozen in position; it was almost possible to feel and smell the fear and uncertainty. The clock of life only restarted when King swung round and bawled 'well, get on with it! Go and wash your miserable dirty selves.' The result was startling, almost as if a fox had suddenly been dropped among a flock of hens. Recruits rushed, dashed and scrambled everywhere and anywhere to get out of King's sight and away from the range of his attention. For them, crowding into the ablutions was like seeking the sanctuary of a church ... but they were no safer there than Thomas a Becket had been in Canterbury cathedral.

The ablutions area consisted of a three-sided room open on the side that was the corridor between the Flights. There were twelve washbasins; six on each of two of the sides. In their haste to get out of King's way, the recruits were packed mostly two to a basin. King strode – he seemed incapable of walking – to the open side of the ablutions area. Behind him marched Corporal Rydall in pyjamas and boots, making an anxious effort to keep in step and behind the Sergeant Major.

'Corporal!' bellowed King.

'Yes, Sarge ... ant Major.' In his anxiety he'd almost forgotten himself. Usually it was acceptable for Corporals to call Sergeants 'Sarge', and Flight Sergeants 'chief' or 'chiefy', but this did not apply to King. He used his rank to keep himself isolated from everyone.

King gave the Corporal a look to show that he had noticed the near slip of the tongue.

'Flight duties for this lot, that one there, and the one by the end washbasin,' said King, pointing to David and Eric. 'Put them on cleaning latrines and the one that's dressed obviously likes to get early ablutions, so put him on ablution cleaning. Him there – floors.' And so he went on detailing various tasks to different recruits.

'The usual weekly rotation of duties, Sergeant Major?' enquired Rydal with what he had hoped was a suitable measure of humility, to avoid any rebuke.

'Did I say so?' asked King with undisguised sneering sarcasm. 'Keep the bogs and ablutions for six weeks and the rest you can put on a ten-day rota.' He knew the ten-day rota would make it much more difficult for Rydal to keep track of, and he could come down on him like a ton of bricks if he got it wrong.

'Right, Sergeant Major.'

Without reply King abruptly turned and marched out of the Flight block, no doubt to go and make life miserable for some other poor sods.

'Thank you for the push out of bed this morning, Jack. I'm not used to getting up this early but I expect that I'll soon become used to it.'

'You won't have much choice, Dave'

There was a fussing of silent activity, everyone listening and half-expecting King to return trying to catch them unawares. After a minute of unuttered but nevertheless heartfelt anxiety, a sigh of relief whispered through the ablution area like the rustling of leaves in a light wind.

'Right – get a move on, you lot.' Corporal Rydal's voice rang through the Flight and consciousness of the young men in the ablution area. 'You heard the Sergeant Major.' He was trying to create the impression that he was an extension of King's authority, but no-one was fooled; they'd seen the way the

Sergeant Major had treated him.

'Breakfast oh seven 'undred prompt, Flight cleaning oh seven-thirty, inspection oh nine 'undred, 'aircuts oh ten 'undred, drill eleven 'undred, and dinner twelve 'undred 'ours. I'll give you the rest of your bleeding programme in the mess 'all. You'd better get a move on or you'll miss breakfast.'

The tempo of movement upped several notches.

'It sounds as if we are going to be quite busy,' said David cheerfully.

'Rushed off our bloody feet is more like it,' said Jack.

'Well we have an hour between the inspection and the check on our haircuts.' David sounded a bit hurt, as if resenting the criticism of the way that things were done in the RAF.

Preparation for the inspection was an eye-opener for all the recruits, including Jack. Their introduction to service life 'bull' was such a revelation that quite a few of them thought that the corporal was 'having them on'.

'Corporal, you're not serious are you? Do we really have to polish the coal shovel and fire bucket?'

'Until you can see your reflection in them,' came the prompt reply. 'Now gather round this bed, you lot, and I'll show you how to fold and lay out your kit.'

The airmen gathered round as instructed, and were introduced to the intricacies of kit arrangement. How to fold blankets, greatcoats, tunics and other paraphernalia so that instead of resembling their normal shapes they looked like a series of boxes. Even Jack, with his experience of sea-going, where space was at a premium and tidiness was essential, was staggered by the lengths to which they were expected to go in the folding, packing and laying-out of their kit.

'Whoever heard of polishing the soles of your boots? Talk about the height of bloody stupidity.'

But that is what they did.

Trying to get the items to sit square and in line, like the demonstration set out by the Corporal, was a nightmare and the rest of the Flight looked with envy at the bed laid out as an example. Everyone wished that it had been their bed that the Corporal had chosen to use for the demonstration. There was much standing back to view attempts at perpendicularity and alignment. The only lighter moment in this frantic period was when a plaintive cry rang out from some despairing soul, after the failure of their umpteenth effort.

'Oh effing hell, it still looks like the bleeding tower of Pisa!'

Even the Corporal laughed.

Ginger's layout was one of the better efforts, but David's, despite the enthusiastic way that he went about the task, left a lot to be desired – so Ginger and Jack gave him a helping hand. Eventually the beds, blankets and lockers were lined up, the floor was polished and everything that could be reached was dusted. To complete the preparations on time turned out to be a frantic rush.

There was not an hour between inspection and haircuts. King's inspections, they soon learned, were a thing of brutality and a pain forever ... well not quite forever, but it did seem like it while they were in progress. He would run his finger along almost inaccessible ledges and then intimidate some poor sod with a thin line of dust on his finger.

'What's that, airman?' King would demand, thrusting his finger under the nostrils of the victim.

'Dust, Sergeant Major.'

'Dust? Dust! It's filth! I suppose you lived in a pig-sty and wallowed in mire before you joined up.'

The first recruit had the sense not to react to the aspersions cast about the cleanliness of his home life and remained silent. Further victims recognised the dust as filth and acknowledged by their silence the alleged disgusting conditions of the homes from which they'd come. The inspection lasted fifty-five minutes, at the end of which the originally reasonably tidy Flight looked as if it had been hit by a hurricane.

Despite the helping hand that Jack and Ginger had given to David, he had ended up as one of the five who were placed on a charge and detailed to present themselves in front of the officer of the watch that evening on defaulters' parade. They were all disappointed at the prospect of 'blotting their copy books', none more so than David. Jack was somewhat surprised not to have been numbered among the 'defaulters'.

Turning to David, in an attempt to console him, he said:

'Never mind Dave, I expect that Ginge and me will get our turn next.'

'Yes but I so wanted to ... keep a clean sheet.'

It was clear to Jack that David had wanted to excel, not just scrape by.

'Don't worry,' he said, 'I don't expect any of the Flight will leave here with a clean sheet.'

That turned out to be a prophetically accurate statement.

As he made his way to the Sergeant's Mess for a cup of tea, King reflected on this latest assault on a set of new recruits. This show of authority over the victims was always tarnished by the knowledge that his married quarters would in no way stand up to any such inspection. He'd long since come to the conclusion that Eunice was, not to put too fine a point on it, a 'mucky bitch'. She only did a minimal amount of housework about once a fortnight. But he knew that the treatment which he regularly meted-out to the recruits would not be tolerated by his wife. Although he didn't have any real affection for her, she was a passably good cook and she was there to meet his needs when he made the occasional foray in to the realms of sexual activity, on which occasions the young lady from Richmond was never far from his thoughts. She was the 'Petal' of his fantasies, the secret 'Betty' of his dreams.

The Sergeant's Mess did not feature highly in the places where he preferred to spend his free time. He couldn't say that he had any real companions there. He was more or less an outcast, and in truth he preferred it that way.

After the inspection, everyone was too demoralised even to complain. It had taken so long that there wasn't even time to tidy up properly before they were marched off for haircuts. This turned out not to be just an inspection of the length of their hair. Even David, who had taken the trouble to get his hair cut short before the journey south, was not as well-informed about the RAF as he thought. Like the rest, he went as a sheep to the shearer. The whole group of them had their hair cut unbelievably short on the sides with peculiarly shaped tufts on the top. One theory was that the barber deliberately went out of his way to make the recruits look ridiculous, under the instructions of Sergeant Major King, as part of a demoralising exercise. Another favoured explanation was that the local barber had an arrangement with the one on the base, because the first thing that new recruits did, when they were allowed off camp, was to visit the village barber and get their hair cut into a less ridiculous shapes.

What started out as a miserable day proceeded to get steadily worse, and by the end of the week, most of the members of 'entry' were wondering how or if they would survive the first month of life in the RAF. They wondered what all the marching and cleaning of kit had to do with being an airman. The reduction in drill and inspections and the start of learning to be air-mechanics seemed to be an eternity away.

The issue of rifles after the first few weeks of drill training was one of the few things that David didn't welcome with his usual enthusiasm. A few members of the Flight seemed to enjoy having the rifles, and there was a certain amount of playing at being soldiers and pretending to be in the trenches. Despite the warnings that they'd been given about not pointing the rifle at one another, the Corporal caught some of them doing just that. His reaction was rather dramatic and it was the closest to him being angry that they ever saw. They were not to discover until much later that his brother had been killed in a shooting accident under similar circumstances. By way of punishment he gave out some extra unpleasant Flight duties to the guilty parties. This was almost the limit of his authority without referring to Sergeant Major King and it seemed as if, even in his anger, he was loath to do that. Those of the Flight who'd welcomed the acquisition of the rifles soon changed their minds when it came to the drill and cleaning of the new issue. The ex-army Lee-Enfields had all seen better days in the Great War, yet King expected the recruits to clean and polish them until they looked like new.

'I must be honest with you, Jack, I am not too keen on guns,' admitted David, as they sat cleaning their rifles that evening.

'Well you don't have to worry about these, Dave. I don't know why Rydal got all worked up with those who were playing soldiers earlier. Remember what the issuing Corporal said – all of these rifles are useless. Their firing pins have all been filed off

– besides which we haven't got any ammunition.'

'You know why that is,' chipped in Ginger. 'Because if we could fire 'em and we did have ammo, some bugger would shoot King. No! On second thoughts, every bugger would shoot that bastard.'

'You really shouldn't say things like that, Ginger,' said David.

Jack knew the direction that this long-running disagreement between David and Ginger was heading.

'Hang on, Dave – you're not still trying to tell me that he treats us the way he does 'cos he thinks it's for our own good?'

'Well yes, I think that he probably does,' said David, colouring-up as usual.

'Never! He treats us this way because he just enjoys being a bastard.'

Before this discussion could continue, Corporal Rydall came up to the group, smiling all over his face.

'You can always catch someone with it,' he said, finding it difficult not to laugh. 'I've sent 'Buller' Brown over to the stores to ask for a long weight for a pull-through.'

They sat looking at the Corporal rather blank for a few moments until the penny dropped.

When 'Buller', who had that nickname because of his habit of telling tall stories, returned about a quarter of an hour later he looked rather sheepish as he handed a normal pull-through to Rydall.

'You had quite a long wait for it, then,' observed the Corporal.

There was a roar of laughter from the Flight. Even the humbled recruit could see the funny side of it and joined in the laughing.

Later, when they were all busy cleaning their kit, Jack said: 'He's alright, that Rydall.'

There was general agreement, even by those to whom the Corporal had given the extra Flight duties.

'Pity they're not all like him,' added Ginger.

Everyone knew who he had in mind when he said that.

CHAPTER SIX

The start of the next day's travelling was delayed for almost half of the time before noon because the bodies had to be disposed of, although none of their spirits were offered to the Sun God.

When the visit to King Solomon had been planned it had been decided to have a contingent of soldiers and bodyguards that was sufficient to provide adequate security for the Queen but not so many soldiers that could be perceived as a small invading force. The loss of seven soldiers plus Ordek was considered acceptable and the Queen's safety was not thought to be compromised. Ordek was replaced by Zeki, one of the senior soldiers. Kariz had had been pleased to help the senior advisor in the selection of this new commander. He had know Zeki for quite a few summers and he knew that he was a reliable, organised soldier who was an adept fighter and would have made a good recruit to the Royal bodyguard.

The journey continued for another three moons of unremitting routine before the next major incident occurred. It was the middle of the day and the ever-present Sun, the one that they worshipped, was making its presence felt, slowly leaching their energy and bleaching their surroundings. Suddenly one of the camels started to become agitated, then another. Soon all the camels appeared to be on edge. Then the guide at the front of the caravan became very animated, pointing to the horizon in the direction that they were heading, and waving frantically. The edge of the sky was rapidly darkening: everyone knew what this meant. A sand storm was racing towards them. The caravan stopped immediately. All the camels were bedded down, the Queen's conveyance was put down and turned so that its solid wall faced the oncoming storm, and the bodyguards assembled with their bedded-down camels around the Queen's conveyance. They just had time to turn their backs to the approaching storm before it struck. The sky soon became as black as night. The still air became a zephyr, a breeze, a storm, and then a blast, all within the time that it took take ten breaths. But this was not the time for taking breaths – this was the time to cover faces, the time to make sure that no parts of parts of the body were exposed to the sand which was being hurled around by a demonic wind. The storm lasted a very long time; usually these storms would disappear as quickly as they appeared, but not on this occasion. When the Sun did eventually re-appear it was nearly halfway to the horizon.

Mounds of sand began to take on the shapes of camels as they were allowed to stand. The bodyguards removed the sand that had piled around the royal conveyance. Once Kariz had made sure that the Queen was safe, the conveyance was moved to more level ground because the caravan had been on the slope of a dune when the sandstorm had struck. Although it was still quite early, the decision was made to set up camp for the night. During the process of moving to a more level site there was a disturbing discovery. The senior guide, who had travelled this trade route almost every year since he was a lad, had been found dead near one of the camels that had been at the forefront of the caravan.

When his body was pulled from underneath the mound of sand where the storm had buried him, it was discovered that he had a small bruise in the middle of his forehead. The senior advisor, who in addition to advising the Queen also dealt with any injured or wounded members of the caravan, decided that the malevolence within the storm had hurled a stone at the senior guide to stun him and then covered him with sand and suffocated him. The guide's body was prepared for the appearance of the Sun God in the morning. The next morning, however, the Sun God failed to appear.

When the time for the dawn arrived there was a blanket of whiteness covering the area. Many of the members of the caravan had never seen anything like it before. A few, including Kariz, who had at some time in their lives been to the coast, knew exactly what it was. When they saw the whiteness they told the rest of the caravan not to worry and that there must be water somewhere nearby. This was very welcome news because it had been many days since the last well and their water supply was becoming worryingly low.

It was not possible to offer the guide's spirit to the Sun God, so a funeral pyre was constructed and lit. It produced an eerie spectacle with the light of the flames reflecting from the whiteness which began to wave and swirl about near the fire. Many of the onlookers, despite having been told about the whiteness, became alarmed almost to the point of panic. It was only the presence of Kariz and his men standing resolutely and unflinchingly erect near the Queen and around the pyre that stopped them from fleeing the scene.

The guide's son and his cousin now had to take on the mantles of 'caravan guides' because they were the only ones that had ever been as far as the 'land of milk and honey'. Unfortunately they had only accompanied the deceased guide on three of his trips. He had been a guide for trade caravans long before either of them had been born. Although they had learnt a little about finding the route by observing the locations of the stars in the heavens, neither of them could be considered competent in reading the stars and their positions to navigate their way across the desert.

Nevertheless, because of the water situation, it was decided to make a start and so the caravan decamped and set off through the whiteness in what was hoped was the correct direction. The sandstorm had obliterated all signs of their previous tracks and it was only later that they discovered they had chosen the wrong direction. The caravan continued journeying until the whiteness began to take on an equally strange darkness. Camp was set up and sentries were posted. It had been a very quiet day of travel; the whiteness distorted voices and swallowed their words and everyone avoided talking.

Halfway through the night watch, one of the sentries woke Zeki and reported that the whiteness had disappeared as quietly and mysteriously as it had appeared. There was a strong bond developing between the commander of the soldiers and the commander of the royal bodyguards. Sending the news to Kariz about the disappearance of the whiteness was almost an automatic reflex for Zeki.

The customary morning worship ritual started as usual but

the Sun God appeared in a slightly different position on the horizon to where the Queen's advisor had expected him to reveal himself. Practically everyone in the caravan realised that the storm had caused them to deviate from the route that they had previously been following. The young, newly appointed, guides immediately pointed in the new direction that should be taken and the caravan set off. It was accepted that it should be the route to follow because the reality was that there was no other choice. The next day they were supposed to reach a well. They didn't. Everyone was very disappointed and thirsty. After two more days they still hadn't reached the well, and the need for water was becoming critical.

The two young guides were doing their best, but whereas the original guide had known the names of every star in the heavens, and how they should be positioned, the youngsters knew only a handful. Nevertheless, even with their limited knowledge, they were well aware that the caravan was lost.

After a further two days the water situation had become desperate. Fate once again took a hand. Just before midday Shahin, the bodyguard who had seen the glint of what had turned out to have been a shiny buckle on one of the of one the brigand's camels, reported to Kariz that he had seen movement on the side of the hill about five thousand paces to the west of the caravan.

In case it was another gang of bandits waiting to attack them, the caravan was halted, and after a brief consultation it was agreed to send a small cohort of six bodyguards and six soldiers to investigate and if necessary deal with any threat. The small contingent set off almost immediately. When they drew near to the place where the movement had been sighted, remaining on their camels, the bodyguards circled to the left and the soldiers to the right. They were only halfway through the manoeuvre when suddenly a small herd of antelope broke cover from the sparse scrub and proceeded to vault and bounce their way down the hill.

'Oh bollocks!' exclaimed one of the soldiers. 'We might have been able to grab a couple of those if we'd been on foot. They would have made a nice addition to the food supplies.'

Any disappointment was short-lived. The front soldier, who was further up the hill, shouted out: 'Come and look'. They all rode up the hill to where he was. He had a broad grin on his face. There in front of him was a large pool of water where the antelopes had been drinking. The now very happy mixed contingent, in a well-disciplined manner, turned their camels – it was not easy turning thirsty camels – and returned to the caravan at a loping trot.

As soon as the information about the pool was received the Queen was informed and the caravan's route was changed. They set off to the west, and well before sunset camp was set up just five hundred paces from the pool. Everyone except the Queen and her attendants was occupied in replenishing the water supplies, filling the water skins and anything else that would hold the precious liquid.

The next morning it felt like a different world. At dawn everyone had paid homage to the Sun God with increased fervour. As there appeared to be no alternative, when the caravan set out that day it followed the same direction as before. For three days they continued on this course during which time, although everyone was being frugal with the water supply, Kariz became increasingly concerned – he could tell from their mannerisms and the looks on the their faces that the young 'guides' were becoming increasingly indecisive about the direction to follow. On the fourth day, just after noon, Shahin reported to Kariz that he thought he could see buildings on the horizon in a gap between the mountains to the west. The news was spread, everyone stared in the direction indicated by Shahin, but no-one else could see anything. It was decision time. Kariz together with Zeki went to see the senior advisor. The commander of the Queen's bodyguards had every confidence in his man: hadn't it been Shahin who had seen the glinting that gave away the position of the brigands, and hadn't he seen the movement that led to the finding of the water? It didn't take much for Kariz to convince the advisor. The caravan's course was changed and they set out for what might be habitation. The caravan had travelled more than two thousand paces before anyone else caught sight of the possible dwellings, but before sunset the number of people confirming the sighting of buildings increased dramatically. The looks on the faces of the young guides reflected their inner relief. Nevertheless, it was almost sunset two days later, because of the difficult terrain, that the caravan arrived at what turned out to be Hegra, one of the main towns on the trade route from the south.

CHAPTER SEVEN

The total and utter misery of the first six weeks of basic training eventually came to an end and they started on the next phase of becoming air mechanics. At long last they were introduced to the workshops, where they came into contact with a completely different kind of NCO. Here the three stripes with a crown signified a Flight Sergeant – these servicemen had been trained and had experience in different trades, and their role was to pass on their skills to the recruits in their charge. A different discipline held sway in the workshops. Here, the important thing was the job. A messy bench or a careless piece of work would receive the same sort of rebuke that the new airmen were accustomed to for incorrectly folded kit. Although their boots, of necessity, were bulled to a 'parade ground shine', the boots of the Flight Sergeants would often be so dulled by oil grease and grime that they looked more like black canvas. On the other hand, tools and equipment were treated like treasured ornaments – these were the pride and joy of all the workshop NCOs, and it would be big trouble for anyone who didn't treat them accordingly.

The enthusiasm with which everyone greeted the start of workshop training was completely unrestrained. The fact that they would see much less of Sergeant Major King had no little bearing on this. Nevertheless they would not be totally beyond his reach until they had completed their training and were posted to some other RAF base. There were still the morning parades, the fatigues, the weekly kit inspections with the resultant defaulters' parades and the frequent ceremonial occasions, all of which, much to everyone's dismay, brought them into contact with King. On these occasions the Sergeant Major went to great lengths to make up for the time that Flight C had been out of his clutches.

Almost every week with monotonous regularity King would find some 'reason' to put David and Eric, the other self-confessed educated member of the Flight, on punishment, known as 'jankers'. But it was not only the regular jankers that made everyone in the Flight think that King had it in for these two; it was the way in which they always seemed to end up with the worst fatigues. The only unpleasant fatigue duty in which Eric outscored David was on the refuse cart, which involved dustbins being taken to the rubbish tip, swill taken to the local pig farm and the pig manure to the camp garden. It was this last task that gave this particular fatigue its descriptive title of 'the shit cart run'. After one particularly exhausting episode on defaulters' parade, just before lights out, David was sitting on his bed taking off his puttees and pulling the boots off his very tired feet. He and Eric had been late again; they were both hungry, having missed another meal and been too late for the NAAFI. Eric had wandered down the Flight and was standing in the space between David's and Jack's beds

'You know what?' he said. 'I've had it with these bloody jankers. I'm sure that that bastard King can't get away with victimising us like this all the time. There's got to be something that we can do.'

'Well I don't know, Eric. Have you considered this – he might be doing it to see if we would make good officer material? Remember the first time we met him ...'

'Bullshit!' Eric interrupted in a weary voice. 'He gives us jankers because he can't stand us being better educated than he is and it gets right up his nose. In fact I've had it with the whole bleeding RAF.'

For a few more minutes, before the lights were put out, they continued their discussion. As Eric was about to make his way back to his bed he whispered to them in a conspiratorial voice: 'I've decided to "work my ticket". Been getting good advice from some of the old hands on the station.'

That evening, he started to set about his task. Each night after 'lights out' he spent about ten minutes hunched up on his bed with his head under the bedclothes, inhaling the smoke from a small piece of smouldering blanket that he had set alight. At the end of three weeks he looked quite ill and legitimately went on sick parade. Two weeks after that he was medically discharged as asthmatic. Several of his fellow recruits considered that what he'd done was damned dangerous.

'Could easily have killed 'iself or burnt the bleeding place down and bloody well killed us all. Stupid bugger,' was the comment passed by the 'erk' in the bed next to Eric.

There were quite a few who envied Eric in his escape from King's clutches.

David repeatedly voiced his opinion that what Eric had done was dreadful. 'Things are not all that bad' he would say, adding, 'it's all done for our own good.' This did not endear him to the rest of the Flight. He kept smiling, but things kept getting worse: there was no let up in King's unfathomable campaign to wear-down David. He was appearing so many times on jankers that even the Flight Lieutenant was getting more than a little fed up with seeing him there.

Time on jankers was miserable, the monotonous full kit inspections and the rapid uniform changes were morale sapping, and the doubling around the parade ground in full kit with a rifle and full backpack was physically exhausting. Although David had a great deal of help from Jack and Ginger and other members of the Flight, he was beginning to show the strain. After a while, David no longer suggested that it was all for his own good.

A new member of the Flight, who had been transferred for retraining from a group that had started six months earlier, heard them talking about the likelihood of David being broken by King's treatment and joined the conversation.

'I can tell you about being broken by NCOs,' he said.

He told them of one of the members of his former Flight who had been caught stealing personal property from other

Flight members. He'd been sent 'over the wall' for twenty-eight days in Aldershot military prison and he'd come back a withdrawn and broken man who was then dishonourably discharged. He'd gone to Aldershot as a hard man. He'd grown up in the Gorbals tenements in Glasgow, and he'd been afraid of nothing and no-one. He'd come back over a stone lighter, afraid of everything and everyone. Even those members of the Flight who had not liked him before he'd been sent to the military prison felt sorry for him when they saw how he had been changed. In the few days before his discharge, he had told his soon-to-be former colleagues about the dreadful conditions and treatment he'd suffered. The waking hours had been filled with misery. Whenever prisoners moved from one place to another it had been done at the double. There had been the exhausting and soul-destroying digging of a hole to fill the hole left by the digging of a hole, left by ... The scrubbing of vast areas of parade ground with toothbrushes had been demoralising and being on your knees for hours on end on the hard ground had been excruciatingly painful. When the 'warders' had tired of seeing the inmates suffering knee pain, they had ordered them to move large packing cases filled with rocks from one side of the parade ground to the other and then back again. This had been back breaking. Their sleeping hours, never more than six, had been filled with the pain of aching muscles and joints, and the aching of shrinking stomachs from the lack of sufficient food. During his time in the military prison, he'd said that one of the inmates had hanged himself from his cell bars with a belt that somehow he'd been able to conceal in his cell. Everyone who heard the tales about what happens 'over the wall' resolved, without exception, that they would never risk doing anything that might get them sent there.

Although King had David up on a charge that would have meant him missing Christmas leave – the first leave for the group, the Flight Lieutenant who heard the charge let David off with a reprimand, much to King's annoyance. They were granted ten days' leave starting on Christmas Eve. They were each given travel warrants and told that they were to be back by 23:59 on Sunday 4 January.

When Jack arrived home in his smart new uniform, the unpleasantness of his leaving was all forgotten. Although his arrival was unexpected, room was made for him, though he had to share a bed with his younger brother. On his way home through London he had managed to buy a small present for each of the family. This time he took care to ask his dad if it would be alright to give the presents to his brother, sisters and mother. The Old Man smiled his approval and smiled even more when Jack handed him a pouch of baccy. It turned out to be just about the best Christmas they could remember.

※

At David's parents' home, his father grilled him about the RAF and then suddenly said: 'I hope you have been behaving yourself, David – not consorting and cavorting with women.'

'No, father,' he stammered.

It was true, except for the fact that David, like all the other young recruits, had suffered the unwelcome and unpleasant touching under the table at the hands – or more accurately the hand – of Eunice, his tormentor's wife. None of them understood why she did it, and they all wondered whether King knew about it. The reality was that King did know about it and took a perverted form of pleasure from it. He knew also that no-one would try anything on with Eunice, simply because she was his wife.

Every Saturday night, when her husband was invariably on duty, she would make her way to the local pub, which was just under a mile away from the 'base'. It was always a mystery why King chose to be on duty on Saturday evenings, but it meant that she could stay in the pub until closing time at 10 o'clock. At about eight o'clock she would make her way to the public bar, dolled-up to the nines, mutton dressed as lamb. Once there, she would try to persuade any unfortunate, even unwilling, victim to buy her a port and lemon. After this she would sidle almost snake-like alongside them and under the table would run her hand along the inside of the thigh of her quarry and ... After living with King for almost ten years she had begun to adopt some of his tormenting ways. They'd heard her say, time and time again: 'You be nice to Eunice (which she pronounced as 'you nice') and Eunice will be nice to you.' Because of Eunice's reputation, many of the men on the base would avoid going to that particular hostelry on a Saturday night. Corporal Rydal had warned Flight C about Saturday nights at the 'local' without naming names. Although Eunice was younger than King, they all thought – quite rightly – that she was old enough to be their mother. She was always careful not to have more than three port and lemons in case anyone tried to take advantage of her.

The topic of conversation with his father changed after that, and David inadvertently let it slip about his frequent appearances on defaulters' parade.

'I am rather disappointed, David, that you have had to be corrected so many times,' said his father sternly. 'Of course, I understand all about this – you have no idea how many times I have had to keep pupils in after school for not paying attention. It has been quite unpleasant when they have had to do lines sometimes for half an hour or more, but it has always been for their own good. This Sergeant Major King sounds like a man after my own heart. You must make more effort to keep in the good books of the Sergeant Major.'

'For their own good? Really?' said David with a face that said 'you have no idea what goes on in the real world' written all over it. He got up from the table.

Silence prevailed, then his father continued, as if David hadn't said anything.

'We do so want you to try a bit harder, David. Your mother and I don't want another disappointment like the matriculation exam, do we? Try to get into the good books of the Sergeant Major.'

'Yes, father,' replied David with his normal automatic response.

❦

When David's great-aunt Maud in Halifax received his Christmas card, a letter fluttered out. He'd always had a close relationship with Maud and been able to confide in her in a way he could not with his stiffly formal father and timid mother, so she was delighted that he'd taken the trouble to write. She was not much older than his mother and, though attractive, had never married, declaring herself an ardent 'man hater' and joining the suffragette movement when she was in her early thirties. She now lived with Violet, whose mannish dress drew a few nudges from her fellow villagers and a lot of speculation about their relationship.

'Violet – I've had a letter from David, but it's not good news. He's trying to sound brave but he is clearly unhappy with the RAF, poor boy. Perhaps we should invite him over at his next leave, to cheer him up a bit?'

'If you want, Maud,' said Violet, never one to particularly cherish the idea of young men about the house.

'I don't think I've ever told you the real story about him, have I?'

'Is it salacious?'

'Well, yes – I suppose it is.'

'Then do tell,' said Violet, putting down her cigarette on the edge of the ashtray.

'It's really about Letty, his mother. She arrived on my doorstep one day – this would have been nearly twenty years ago now – clutching a letter from my sister. This letter said that I was their last hope. Letty had got pregnant by some young soldier she'd met – apparently she didn't even know the man's name. Damnation on him, taking advantage of her innocence like that! My sister just wanted rid of the whole business and thought I could deal with it.'

'What on earth did you do? Did she stay with you through her confinement?'

'No – I thought of a better way,' said Maud. 'She was less than two months' gone and it didn't show. So I arranged a little seduction.'

'What do you mean?'

'I invited a family from Cedar Avenue to a soiree for young people – they were to send their son, Lancelot, along.'

'Lancelot White?' cried Violet in amazement.

'The very same. I tutored Letty on how to seduce Lancelot. It worked perfectly. At their second meeting, they were left unchaperoned for a while. And soon after that, Letty declared herself to be with child; a hasty wedding was arranged; the scandal was buried; and baby David was born seven months later.'

'And Lancelot never guessed?'

'Men are such dullards. He never did work out that the timing was all wrong.'

'And she's had to suffer being married to him all these years?'

'That was the price that dear Letty had to pay, I'm afraid.'

*

King had what he considered one of his worst Christmases ever. They had spent it at his sister-in-law's house in Broadstairs. He and Eunice had no children and Eunice had always blamed that on him: her sister and brother-in-law had three boys. King had always wanted a son, and he was bitterly disappointed that Eunice had never joined the pudding club. He knew that if he had fathered a son his offspring would have been one to be proud of; he would have helped the child to excel in everything. Instead he had to listen to his in-laws going on and on about their brats. It seemed that every conversation came round to them talking about the boys and how well they were doing at school and college, and how their *education* was making them blossom. Henry King was quite pleased to get back to Manston after the Christmas leave. Surprisingly most of the members of the Flight were also pleased to be back, though it was noticeable that David seemed to have lost much of his enthusiasm.

King didn't waste any time in getting back to his vindictive, bullying ways. David, despite his increased efforts to perform well, quickly resumed his regular appearance on jankers. It was during the first week of February, in the evening, when David was on defaulters' parade that one of the members of the Flight who was helping to sort out some kit on David's bed, turned to Jack and said: 'Look Jack, you're his mucker – if we don't do something soon about young Dave' – it was odd how everyone referred to him as young Dave – 'he's going to effing well break. Can't we go and see the CO and put him in the ...'

'There's no way we can get to the CO without going

through King,' said Jack. 'Even if we could, the CO wouldn't do anything – he'd be bound to take King's side and then that bastard would take it out on us all, but most of all on Dave.'

'Yeah, I know you're right, Jack, but it's bloody hard to stand by and watch King pick on the kid, especially as he don't deserve it. I'm sure young Dave's going to break.'

These words turned out to be prophetic.

It was only two weeks later during the next big inspection that it happened. King had now become quite blatant in his victimisation. Once again he had demolished David's quite passable kit layout. David stood there in the wreckage of all his hard work with the likelihood of more totally undeserved jankers hanging over his head, and any chance of him pleasing his mother and father blown away. Not by a gentle breeze but by a vicious hurricane. He reached down and took the eighteen-inch bayonet out of its scabbard and threw it at the Sergeant Major. It was a despairing petulant act of defiance rather than a serious attempt at injuring King. His voice edged with open emotion, David – almost in tears – blurted out: 'My kit was correct .... you're just picking on me just because you don't like me.'

The silence in the Flight took on a cloak of expectancy, as the two dozen or so men who were standing at attention held their breaths. They knew that a new drama was about to be played out before them. *'Oh you damned fool, Dave,'* thought Jack, *'can't you see you've played right into his hands?'*

'Yes, you bastard, you're just picking on him,' he said out loud.

King ignored Jack and turned towards David slowly and deliberately, like a lion stalking a young antelope. He knew that he'd won before he even pounced.

'So you'd try to kill me, would you, White? You with all your high and mighty ways and education.'

David looked terrified

'Don't be so bloody stupid, King,' shouted out Jack, taking a pace forward in the time-honoured fashion in an attempt to interrupt.

'And you can be quiet, Toulson. I'll deal with you later.'

Jack realised there was no point in saying any more, but

he did not take the customary step back. King ignored this. What happened next made Jack bitterly sorry that he had said anything at all. Acting on this support from his best friend, David leapt forward, grabbed the fallen bayonet and lunged at King who swayed to one side to avoid the charge and, with ridiculous ease took the bayonet from the would-be assailant. Throughout the whole fiasco the triumphant look never left King's face. David now burst into uncontrolled tears of frustration, shame and fear. The silence in the room changed from expectation to embarrassment.

'Right, Corporal – arrest Airman White and take him to the guardhouse.'

Rydal knew that the RAF police duty NCO should have been summoned, but he was not about to argue with King. He moved alongside David and gently took him by the arm.

'That's no way to handle a criminal, Rydal. Grab hold of him and use any necessary force,' bellowed King.

Rydal took a firmer hold on David, but the look on his face showed the contempt that he had for King.

'You're supposed to be a disciplined NCO, Corporal, so go about your duties correctly or you'll find yourself back in the ranks. You saw how he attacked me.'

Rydal didn't say anything to King but turned to David instead.

'C'mon, lad, let's go.' They marched off to the guardhouse.

'Remember I'll deal with you later,' said King to Jack. 'And you won't be so ready to mouth off after it.'

The Sergeant Major had decided that it would be a good idea to let Jack stew for a while. *'That'll teach 'im,'* thought King.

But the delay was to prove to be a significant error.

The inspection was now long forgotten. Instead of the usual relieved hubbub of chat that signalled the departure of the Sergeant Major, this time there was a solemn and depressed silence that hung in the Flight like a morning mist over a marsh, as the airmen set about the task of putting away their various items of kit.

The silence was partially broken by Gus, one of the Flight who was standing next to Jack.

'A spell over the wall will kill 'im, Jack, it really will.'

'You don't need to tell me that.'

'He seems to have lost nearly all his enthusiasm since Christmas. I could cheerfully kill King for what he's been doing to young Dave. Can't we go and see the CO and put him in the picture?' asked Gus.

'No point,' said Jack. 'We've been over this all before. We would have to go through bloody channels and that means through King.'

'Can't we bypass him some bleeding way?'

'Look, if there was the slightest chance I would bloody well have had a go myself, but there's no way, and the CO wouldn't take any notice of me with the number of times that I've been on jankers – he probably already thinks I'm a trouble-maker.'

'How about if a group of us goes to see the CO?'

'That's no bloody good either – if we go as a deputation it would almost certainly be treated as mutiny. We're knackered whichever way we turn. No, we're buggered whatever we try.'

They all sat gloomily in the Flight despite the prospect of a 72-hour pass in the near future.

'After lights out, I'm going to sneak round the back of the guardhouse to see if I can find Dave and try to cheer him up,' said Jack. 'I don't suppose it'll do much good.' He sounded weary and resigned.

Gus and Ginger immediately volunteered to go with him, to help 'young Dave'. It was well after lights out and getting on towards 11 o'clock when they made their way to the back of the guardhouse. As they were quietly sneaking around a corner of the building Gus tripped over a dustbin and they were caught by the duty Corporal MP. There was no point in making a run for it, so they just stood there until they were ushered into the guardhouse to be dealt with. The Corporal was on duty on his own because three of his five other companions had been called away to help with a large movement of personnel in London, and the other two were off duty until the next day, so he proceeded to take down their names and numbers and to ask them 'what the effing 'ell' they thought they were up to. When they explained what they were trying to do – there was no point in lying to him – to their utter amazement he said OK.

They didn't discover until much later that, during the

previous year, King had almost caused this Corporal to lose his stripes when he'd questioned some action King had taken against another recruit, causing him to be discharged from the RAF. The Corporal recognised the Sergeant Major as a vindictive bully and had said so. To put it mildly, the Corporal hated King's guts. So as an act of retaliation, he let the small group in to see David.

'Keep it quiet lads,' pleaded the Corporal. 'If King finds out that I let you in, he'll have my guts for garters and my stripes as well, this time.'

'How's it going then, Dave?' asked Jack.

David, with his knees pulled into his chest, was squatting on the bunk with his back against the wall. He looked up with the eyes of a hunted animal.

'King's been in to see me. He reminded me of what happened to those who go over the wall. He said that I'll get at least 56 days. Help me Jack ... please, I couldn't face that.'

'Take it easy, Dave – that bastard was only trying to frighten you.'

'But will I, Jack? Will I?'

David's question and the look on his face made Jack regret coming to the guardhouse. He knew that even when the truth hurts, it has to be faced – he couldn't build up false hopes in young Dave, yet if he were to tell him the truth it would make matters worse, much worse. Almost as if sensing Jack's dilemma, one of the others chipped in with a well-timed lie. Gently putting his hand on David's shoulder he said:

'Now what's all this? We're not sure whether the CO will send you over the wall, and if he does we reckon it'll be seven days, or fourteen at the most. Don't forget we're all your mates and we'll back you up.'

It seemed give a little relief to David. A few goodies were produced. A bar of chocolate, a packet of Woodbines, and David's writing pad and envelope that Jack had brought along, together with an indelible pencil.

'Just in case you get time to write and let us know that you are OK,' said Jack. 'But you'd better hide these bits away from you know who.'

Then a silence fell upon the group, the kind of silence that is familiar to all hospital patients at visiting time.

Suddenly they all heard the all-too-familiar sound of studded boots clicking their way towards them, and the 'devil incarnate' was already on the steps outside the guardhouse. The 'visitors' flattened themselves against the walls to get in the shadows, but each of them felt as if they were in the footlights on the stage at the Hippodrome. The door was opened almost with theatrical slowness. The Corporal snapped to attention.

'All present and correct, Sergeant Major,' he said. 'But I would like to report that I feel unwell and not fit to continue guard duty.'

This last statement was perfectly accurate, as the Sergeant Major could clearly see.

'Oh dear me, Corporal,' started King in his usual sarcastic tone. 'I don't know what the services are coming to. No backbone, no guts and no stamina.' Normally he would have left the Corporal, sick or not, to complete his duty but suddenly he had a thought. 'I'll go and detail someone to relieve you,' he said.

He was so pleased with the piece of nastiness he'd thought up that he failed to see the men half hidden in the cell. He turned and stomped of on his new mission, to wake up Rydal who had only finished duty about three hours ago and would have had less than two hours' sleep.

As soon as they were sure that King was well out of earshot, the small group thanked the Corporal and slipped out of the guardhouse.

'Bleeding Hell! He was good, that Corporal. But I bet he nearly shit himself,' said Jack.

'Never mind the Corporal,' said Gus, 'I'm not sure that I haven't.'

Although they were all relieved at not being caught by King, in the guardhouse or on their way back, it had been a nerve-racking episode. After they had crept back into the Flight and into their beds, each of them lay awake for a long time, haunted by the look on David's face when they had left him.

After all the happenings on the Friday night, Saturday morning fatigues were conducted in what appeared to be a mesmerised state. The fatigues came and went in a blur. Just after midday Ginger rushed into the Flight.

'He's gone AWOL!' he shouted.
'What? Dave?' Jack leapt up in alarm.
'Yes Jack, he's done a runner.'
'Oh bloody hell! How did he get out?'
'Rydal reckons that King deliberately let him out.' …

※

After King had left the Corporal MP that night, he had gone to Corporal Rydal's quarters – the room at the end of the Flight C. If he had put on the light in the Flight he would have seen the three empty beds, and the futures of many men, including him, would have been very different – but he hadn't. He had gone straight into Rydal's room, woke him and told him to make his way to the guardhouse and relieve the Corporal who has been taken ill. *'That'll teach him to look at me like he did,'* King had thought. Although Rydal had been still half asleep, he'd got dressed and accompanied King to the guardhouse. Fortunately King's marching footsteps had been neither quiet nor unmistakable and it had given the returning trio time to take cover before he reached them, and they'd managed to get back to the Flight without any problems.

When King, with Rydal in tow, had arrived at the guardhouse, he'd informed the Corporal – who by then didn't look so ill – that Rydal would take over the rest of his duty, and he 'himself' would sort the changes that would have to be made to the duty roster with his Sergeant, when the contingent returned from London. The MP who was being relieved had known very well from what he was saying – and the way that he was saying it – that King was going to make trouble for him again. So in a small act of defiance he had come to attention and said 'Right Sarge!', turned and left the guardroom. Although irritated, Sergeant Major King had been quite pleased because everything was working out just as he'd hoped.

'Right, Corporal. I'll just go and see that the prisoner is OK,' he'd said, taking the key to the cell. He'd gone to the back of the guardroom, unlocked the door and gone in to talk to David. After about ten minutes he'd come back.

'I've left the cell door open,' he'd said. 'Our little educated gentleman's not going anywhere. You don't need to close it.

Rydal must have wondered what the devious bugger was up to, but he wasn't going to argue with King. '

'It's midnight, so I'm going off duty now, Corporal.'

'Right, Sergeant Major.'

It was a mystery which no-one had ever fathomed – why King organised his rota so that he was on duty until midnight on Fridays, Saturdays and Sundays.

As King had made his way back to Married Quarters, he'd smiled to himself at the thought of a job well done. No stuck-up 'educated' raw recruit was going to get the better of him. He had realised that White might not get much more than a month's jankers for throwing that bayonet. *'He'll run, I'm sure of that,'* he thought. What had made him so sure was the look on David's face when he'd reminded him of the stories told by the recruit from Glasgow who'd been sent to Aldershot. *'If he goes AWOL after what he's done, he'll certainly go over the wall.'*

King had been right, because at about two o'clock in the morning Rydal, despite his best efforts, had fallen asleep. David had gathered up his few belongings and slipped quietly out of the guardhouse and set off in the direction of Birchington. It was the last week in February and there was a cold east wind, with a keen edge on it blowing across Thanet. Fortunately it was dry but David must have wished that he'd had his greatcoat with him.

❧

'Why the sodding hell would King let him out?' said Ginger, looking at Jack.

'Why the hell does that bastard do half the things he does?'

Small groups in the Flight sat around talking about this latest development for quite some time. Jack sat on his bed in silent thought for over half an hour.

'Can you cover for me until tomorrow night, Ginge?' he asked, suddenly getting to his feet and purposefully putting on his best blue jacket and greatcoat.

'Yeah, sure Jack – at least I'll do my best. But where are

you going?'

'I think I know where he's gone, I'm going to try to bring him back. Maybe we can then try to make it look as if he never did a bunk. See you soon and thanks.'

'Right'o, Jack – good luck. You'd better be careful! Don't forget the civvy police will already have been alerted. Let's hope you find him before the MPs get him.'

'Do you want any of us to come with you?' called out Gus.

'No thanks, it'll be easier if I go on my own,' Jack called back, and with that he was off.

With so many people coming and going, slipping out of camp without a pass on a Saturday was fairly easy.

Once clear of the camp, Jack made his way to Ramsgate to catch a train to Canterbury, but to his dismay he discovered that there were problems with the trains and he would have to use the buses to get to where he was pretty certain David had gone. When he eventually arrived in Canterbury it was already dark and all the buses to Whitstable had stopped running, so he took shelter in a small church. A railway station, he decided, would be a bit too risky. The local constabulary would, in all probability, be keeping an eye on those. *'They'll think he'll make for London and then try to get home by train,'* thought Jack.

It was an uncomfortable and cold night for Jack, but he did get some sleep. With so few buses running on Sunday, it was after mid-morning before he alighted, unshaven and feeling rather scruffy from his journey, from a nearly empty bus, on this the last stage of his journey. There were only a few people about. Jack guessed that most of them were making their way home after church. The first couple that he spoke to were unable to help, but the next person just happened to be the local postman, dressed in his Sunday best and on his way home from church like the others. He was able to give Jack detailed directions.

※

'Well well, look who's here, George? We knew you'd come as well,' said Esme.

The words 'as well' told Jack that he'd been right in figuring out where Dave would run to.

'It's nice to see you again, Esme – and you, George – but where is he? You know he's in trouble don't you?'

'Well we guessed that something was wrong,' said George, 'but he wouldn't tell us what. He arrived here very early yesterday morning on the milk cart that collects our milk. He asked us to hide him somewhere.' He paused, and then continued. 'What's he done?'

'He don't strike us as the sort who'd get into trouble,' said Esme.

'He's gone AWOL,' said Jack.

'It won't do him any good going on the run. They'll catch him sooner or later and it will only make matters worse.'

'I know, George, I know. That's why I've come to try to take him back.'

'But why is he on the run?'

'It's a long story, and it's not his fault but he's done a runner because he's terrified of going to Aldershot Military Prison.'

'Strewth, Jack, I don't envy you ... taking him back seems hard, but it's the only thing that can be done. It'll be much better if he goes back with you rather than with the red-caps.'

'I tell you, George – I'm not enjoying this one little bit.' As Jack was talking, he caught sight of the nappies airing in front of the range stove.

'Oh, I'm sorry – I forgot ask about your baby. What did you have, a little boy or girl?'

'A little girl,' said Esme excitedly. 'She's fine, she was born on my birthday, and we called her Mary after my mother – she's nearly four months old now. Would you like to see her?' Then, seeing Jack's anxious face, she added 'perhaps you'd better go and fetch David first, then you both can come in and see young Mary. He hasn't seen the baby yet – he's been down in the barn since he got here yesterday. George took him some food yesterday, but we haven't seen him today.'

'Yes, that would be best, Esme,' said Jack. 'We both said that we would come to visit you, didn't we? I just wish it had been under happier circumstances. Anyhow, let's go and fetch Dave first.'

'Won't be a mo, Es,' called out George as he went out with Jack.

'You must stay for a bite to eat before you go back,' Esme called out after them as George and Jack set off down the path.

'He's up in the Dutch barn at the end of the lane. I told him that he could have stayed in the cottage, but he said that he would feel safer in an outbuilding.'

George stopped by the barn. 'He'll be at the back there. It's a good hiding place. They'd never find 'im unless they was looking for 'im with dogs.'

'Wouldn't put that past 'em, George,' he said softly. Then, calling out, he said: 'Hello, Dave – it's me. Where are you? We've got to have a talk'.

He waited for a while. 'Come on, Dave, don't piss about. There's only me and George here. We haven't got a lot of time. Esme wants us to see the baby'.

Jack waited again. Still there was no reply.

'I don't know what he's playing at, George, I expect he's scared – I'll go in and find him.'

'I'll come in with you, Jack. I know where he'll be hiding.'

※

When Esme saw George in the kitchen doorway, head bowed and white-faced, she cried out: 'What's up, George? What's the matter?'

'It's young David, 'e's 'ung 'imself.'

'Oh no! Oh no! Why?'

'As Jack said, he was just terrified of the idea of going to the Military Prison.'

'But he was such a nice young man. I just don't understand, it just don't seem right.'

'We've cut 'im down and Jack's with 'im at the moment. 'E's taken it real bad. We'd better leave 'im alone for a while. I'll 'ave to go and fetch the constable from the village. I'll be back as quick as I can.'

When Jack came back to the cottage he was frighteningly calm. His eyes had a new and even harder depth.

'I'll kill the bastard,' he muttered.

'Who's that, Jack?' said Esme.

'The one that drove Dave to do it.'

67

'Calm down, that won't do any good. You'll only end up on the end of a rope like poor young David if you do.'

She put her hands to her face, her cheeks suddenly colouring when she realised how lacking in tact her words had been. 'David wouldn't want you getting into trouble now, would he?'

'No, I guess you're right, Esme, but I will make the bugg ... the blighter pay for this, he's not going to get away scot free.' He swallowed hard, partly in sorrow, partly in anger.

Jack could tell from Esme's voice that she was on the verge of tears, and was just managing to hold them at bay. He was surprised by the way in which she was coping with the situation. She appeared to be so different from the first impression that he'd had of her on the train. She was more forthcoming, more confident, and definitely much less worried looking. Motherhood suited her. Coming south had worked out well for them, but for young David, for whom it had seemed so promising, it had all turned out so disastrously wrong. For Jack himself it hadn't proved to be too brilliant either.

'I'll make him wish he'd never been born, Sergeant Major or not, so help me God.' Jack said this with the gravity of a judge passing the death sentence on a convicted murderer.

Jack was shown the baby and said all the appropriate things about the father's nose and the mother's eyes. In fact the baby was a particularly cheerful, pleasant and contented looking infant, and Jack was able to compliment them about their little daughter quite truthfully. Remembering a custom of his father's, he pressed a florin into the baby's hand.

'May tha ne'er be wi'out throughout tha life,' recited Jack with an almost religious solemnity. 'She'll be all reet, Esme – did tha see how she grasped t' coin?' he said, lapsing back into the accent of his birth.

'Thank you, Jack, but you shouldn't have ...'

'Nonsense, Esme, it was my pleasure.'

While they were waiting for George to return with the constable, they sat drinking cups of tea and eating a hastily prepared snack.

'This is delicious, Esme – it's the best that I've had to eat for months and months.' The fact that Jack hadn't eaten for nearly twenty-four hours made the meal doubly enjoyable. Although they talked about a number of things, they both knew that eventually they would have to come back to talking about poor young David.

'... Well you see, Esme, he knew that his parents would not be able to stand the shame if he had gone into the Military Prison.'

'I can well imagine that. He struck me as being ever so sensitive and fond of his parents,' said Esme.

'Oh yes he was that, he was very close to his mother. He'd persuaded me to go with him to Halifax to see his parents to explain that it was not his fault that he kept ending up on defaulters' parade. We were going there next weekend to see them. We'd worked like stink to make sure that we would be able to go, and then this ... this ... Sergeant Major deliberately stopped us. Dave just couldn't take any more and he cracked up.'

'Oh Jack, that's awful – how could anyone be like that?'

'I know, Esme. There's some bl ... blooming rotten people in this world.'

Jack thought back to all the dreams that Dave had cherished, of the two of them sharing exciting careers in the RAF. How enthusiastically he'd taken on the challenge, then how progressively squeezed out of him that enthusiasm had been by King. *Why? Why?* There seemed to be no reason why King, right from that very first day, should have picked on Dave.

Just then they heard George coming down the path with the constable. Although Jack knew that he would end up in more trouble than he already was, he had not considered the thought of leaving Dave alone, despite the fact that he was dead. George led the way down to the barn, and showed David's body to the constable.

'I cut 'im down, constable,' said Jack. 'I could see that 'e'd been dead some time.'

'Well you shouldn't really have done that you know,' replied the policeman.

Jack pursed his lips and breathed out heavily through his nostrils, and looked icily at the officer of the law. 'He was my friend and I wasn't bloody well going to leave 'im hanging there.'

The constable looked at Jack's eyes.

'Yes, well that's quite understandable in that case, sir. We will, of course, have to get a doctor to look at him, but it looks as if he did it sometime last night.'

Jack didn't mention the fact that he had found a letter addressed to him from Dave.

The doctor was duly summoned together with a police sergeant and an inspector. Jack explained about David being on the run. After a few more questions, the military police were sent for. Jack was arrested and escorted back to Manston. Much to his surprise he wasn't even detained in the guardhouse, but a record of his being off the camp was noted and then he was allowed to return to the Flight.

By the time that Jack had been returned to the 'fold', the news of David's death was already known by everyone on the base. The members of Flight C were in a state of shock, and nearly as upset as Jack was. Gus, acting as spokesman for them all, came and sat on the end of Jack's bed.

'We're all upset about young Dave, Jack, so we'd like to say how sorry we are about what's happened.'

'Yeah, thanks, Gus – thank you all.'

As he lay on his bed he suddenly realised how tired he was from all the activity and the limited amount of sleep that he'd had the night before. He tried to work out a way make King pay for what he had done and it was almost as if the other lads had read his mind. This time it was Ginger's turn to act as spokesman. He sat on the end of Jack's bed alongside Gus.

'We know how you feel, Jack, but don't do anything stupid – that bastard's not worth it.'

'Don't worry, Ginge, I'll do something but it won't be stupid, mark my words on it, it won't.'

CHAPTER EIGHT

No sooner had Solomon received the Queen of Sheba's reply than he had building work started on a facility to house her when she arrived. He had most of his slave labour taken from the numerous other building projects that were taking place in Jerusalem. Not being one to leave anything to chance, Solomon then summoned Fariq – one of his trusted army commanders – and instructed him to assemble a small group of men. They were to travel to Hegra, a town on the trade route from the south, and await the arrival of the Queen's retinue. They were not to make themselves known as part of King Solomon's army, but to pretend to be traders. When the Queen's party arrived, their role was to mingle with members of the caravan, gather as much information as possible and then return to Jerusalem.

That evening, Fariq set out with six men and waited at Hegra for almost two moons until the arrival of the caravan.

On the evening of its arrival, the caravan from Sheba camped on the outskirts of the town. That evening the atmosphere within the camp was one of exhilaration, all the personal fears and misgivings of the past ten days having dispersed in a similar manner to the lifting of the whiteness out in the desert. There were about seven or eight hundred inhabitants in Hegra and there appeared to be at least ten different wells. As they had approached the town they had come across three separate herds of goats with their goatherds, and had passed a number of olive groves and vineyards.

The caravan stayed in Hegra for two days replenishing their supplies, resting the camels and refreshing the spirit of all.

Before sunrise on the morning that the caravan left Hegra, Fariq and his men quietly set off from where they were camped just to the north of the town, heading for Jerusalem and arriving there ten days later.

Fariq went immediately to see the King, who cancelled all of his other business in order to hear Fariq's report.

'Well what did you discover?' asked Solomon impatiently – he may have been full of wisdom, but he was empty of patience.

'Your majesty, the first thing that we observed was that the Queen worships the Sun, and every morning the complete caravan ...'

'Do they worship idols?'

'Not the Queen, but some of her subjects do, according to what one of my men overheard a woman from the caravan telling a stallholder in the market at Hegra.'

Fariq then went on to report something that startled Solomon.

'The woman was also heard to say to the stallholder – when they were gossiping about the Queen – that for all of her wealth she has hairy legs and a foot like a goat. I also heard mentioned a foot like a goat when one of the Queen's personal maids was laughing about some incident with another member of the caravan'.

The reporting commander went on to detail what they had learned about the caravan being attacked by brigands and then getting lost after a sandstorm and nearly running out of water. The fact that Solomon wasn't listening was apparent, because he had stopped interrupting.

As soon as he had dismissed Fariq, King Solomon ordered that Akil should be brought to him immediately.

When Akil entered the throne room he could see that all was not well; the King was obviously furious.

'What is this that I hear – that the Queen of Sheba has hairy legs and a foot like a goat?' Solomon demanded.

'Your majesty, I didn't ...'

'You said that she was one of the most beautiful women in creation.'

'But, your majesty, there was no ...'

'It's no wonder that there isn't a King of Sheba! This most important piece of information was supposed to have been discovered by you.'

'There was no mention of...'

'If this becomes common knowledge I will not be known for passing good judgements, I will be ridiculed for inviting her here.' With this Solomon ordered one of his bodyguards to take Akil away and have him put in a dungeon. *'I don't want to set eyes on him ever again'.*

Having vented his anger on Akil, Solomon began to work out a strategy to minimise the effect that this recent revelation, if it proved to be true, would have on his reputation. He decided that he had first to verify the hairy legs and goat's foot report; he very quickly came up with a plan. The Queen would no doubt be wearing long garments covering her down to the ground and so her feet would not be visible. He summoned the master builder who was in charge of the slaves that had just completed the semi-palace where the Queen and her retinue were to be accommodated.

'I want you to change the reception hall where I will welcome the Queen. You are to make all of the floor area in the hall into a shallow pool, about a hand's span deep.'

The puzzled master builder was told to repeat back to Solomon the instruction. Following this he was informed that he had three days to complete the task, and was then sent, with a dismissive hand gesture, to go and get the job done.

Even doubling the number of slaves working on the palace, the deadline meant that work had to continue through the nights. Nevertheless the construction of the pool was completed on time.

If the report about the goat's foot was accurate Solomon decided that the Queen of Sheba's reign would have to become shortened, and end before she left Jerusalem.

❦

As the caravan set off from Hegra, everyone in the Queen's entourage were feeling quite elated, perhaps with the exception of Kariz who had a sense of misgiving about something that he had seen but was not quite sure what it was.

Tabuk, the next town on the trade route, came and went

without any undue mishaps. The bodyguard wounded during the brigands' attempted robbery had recovered sufficiently to resume his normal duties. Within seven days they were at the edge of the 'fertile crescent' and with so much more vegetation and more green filling the landscape, it was as if the plants were sucking the arid dust out of the air. Spirits were lifted to an almost euphoric level – even the undefined misgivings that had previously troubled Kariz were pushed to the back of his mind.

Two days later they arrived in Jerusalem. There were different kinds of dark green trees as well as the familiar palms, with wells and water everywhere. It was a much bigger town than any of them had imagined. Everyone was truly awestruck.

As they approached the city gate, the caravan was met by about four hundred troops dressed in uniforms which glistened in the sunlight, because many parts of their regalia were covered with gold. They were mounted on horses that also had trappings covered in gold. 'Horses are alright here,' thought Kariz, 'but not so good in the desert.' He had been brought up with, and had lived with camels, all of his life. The troops escorted the caravan to the facility that had been prepared for them, in the centre of which was the palace where the Queen of Sheba would be housed during her stay. The sides of the roads – and these really were roads – were lined with people, many of them children, who waved as the caravan and escort passed by.

When they arrived at their destination, the Queen's soldiers dismounted and lined up outside the palace. Zeki was quite pleased that the escort had returned to their quarters because his own men would have looked very shabby alongside the resplendent guard of honour. Kariz and the bodyguards also dismounted, handed the reins of their camels to attendants and mustered around the Queen's carriage. The Queen stepped down from her conveyance. Together with her senior advisor and two personal attendants, three bodyguards and Kariz she went into the palace that had been prepared for her. She had been informed it was where she would be received by the King.

Nothing could have prepared any of them for the bizarre scene that was about to unfold. As the large doors to the reception hall were opened, they saw at the far end what was obviously King Solomon dressed in splendid robes, sitting on a golden throne on an elevated dais, with attendants on either side of him. That of course, was more or less what they had expected, however instead of a marbled or carpeted floor, the entire space between the dais and the door consisted of a shallow pool.

'He must have immense wealth to have so much water inside a palace just to freshen the air,' thought the Queen. The rest of her retinue was equally impressed at the demonstration of so much wealth. King Solomon beckoned the Queen to approach. There was some hesitation then, following a hand gesture from her majesty, the two handmaids moved close to the Queen on either side, lifted her robe, removed her sandals and then their own, and together they stepped down into the water.

'She doesn't have a goat's foot or hairy legs and it's true she must be the most beautiful woman in creation.' *This thought of King Solomon was reflected in his face; he became quite wide-eyed. Kariz noticed this. As usual when guarding the Queen in company, he scrutinised the faces of everyone in her immediate vicinity. The face of one of the men on the left hand of Solomon, obviously one of his senior army personnel, immediately struck a chord and it now became clear to Kariz why he had been so troubled with apprehensive thoughts. He'd seen this man before, when the caravan had been in Hegra.* 'I knew he wasn't a trader – he didn't stand or talk like one,' *he thought. Kariz wasn't sure whether it represented a threat or not. Just in case, he made a mental note to make doubly sure that a careful watch was kept on this individual during the Queen's stay in Jerusalem.*

The Queen was invited up on to the dais to a throne alongside Solomon while the rest of her retinue remained standing in the scented water. The welcoming went very well. King Solomon and the Queen of Sheba seemed to be well attuned to each other and the talking went on for some while. For those standing in water for a long time it was not an unpleasant experience after the long dusty journey. Eventually the welcoming ritual was complete. The Queen's attendants moved to one side to allow the King and his attendants to pass, but the King turned and with his entourage left by a door on the right hand side of the dais. They didn't have to pass through the water.

When the King had departed the Queen beckoned her handmaids, bodyguards and advisor onto the dais. Then with

Kariz and his men leading the way – to make sure that everything was safe – they proceeded into the rest of the palace. Kariz sent two of his men ahead to check every room. Apart from the Queen's rooms there were rooms for the advisor, the handmaids, Kariz and another for four bodyguards – two were to be posted outside the Queen's rooms at all times when she was in residence. As soon as the Queen was safely ensconced, Kariz made his way back with the remaining bodyguard to the facility where the rest of his men were to be housed.

'Well that was donkey odd,' said the bodyguard to his commander on the short walk back. Kariz had to agree with him.

'The military man, on the left hand of Solomon – did you recognise him?' Kariz asked.

'No I didn't, but he was vaguely familiar.'

'Well he was in Hegra when we were there, and he was pretending to be a trader. He was asking lots of questions about the Queen and the caravan. I want you to find out about him, and keep an eye on him when you can. He's obviously a spy for the King. I want you to make that your primary assignment during our stay.'

'Right, commander – you can count on me.'

'I know that, otherwise you wouldn't be a Queen's bodyguard.'

That evening King Solomon was contemplating taking himself another wife and the thought occurred to him that Akil had really done a good job, so he summoned the dungeon keeper.

'You can release the prisoner Akil and have him brought to the palace.'

'But your majesty,' said the prison commander in a trembling voice, 'when you said that you didn't ever want to set eyes on him ever again, we thought you meant to despatch him, and we have already done so.'

'Oh!' said the King. 'In that case, see the treasurer and have a purse of gold sent to his widow and family.'

When the widow received the purse of gold she had been grieving for only a few days. She didn't know why Akil had been executed, but she was sure that it was for some good reason; she trusted King Solomon's judgement. Hadn't he been right when he returned her baby son to her despite that other woman claiming that it was her baby and would have cheerfully had him chopped in half? No – she trusted Solomon. Nevertheless Akil had been a good

76

husband; he had married her, an ex-prostitute with a baby which he'd brought up and cared for as his own. This son was now the only male in the household with his mother and three sisters. Next year he was to start service for the King in his army, so the gold from Solomon was a Godsend. She knew that Akil had been handsomely rewarded for the trip before the last one because he had accidently mentioned it when he had been drinking and celebrating his good luck. He must have hidden it somewhere in the house, but she and her three daughters had searched high and low throughout the house for days without success.

Because of Akil's former position in King Solomon's court the family had achieved a good standing in the community, and she dreaded the thought of what might become of them when her son went to be a soldier. The thought of her daughters following in their mother's footsteps was to keep her awake for many nights in the future.

CHAPTER NINE

The Commanding Officer surprised Jack on the Monday evening when he was hauled up on defaulters' parade. The CO actually stood up to the Sergeant Major.

The death of David had not kindled even the slightest hint of remorse or regret in King. In a matter-of-fact voice he rattled out the charges against Jack: insubordination and swearing at an NCO, absence from the base without leave. Then, out of the blue, 'and inciting a prisoner to abscond.' Jack didn't even flinch.

'What have you got to say for yourself, Airman Toulson?' asked the CO.

'Guilty to the insubordination and swearing and the absence without leave charges. Not guilty to the incitement charge, sir'.

The CO sat with his right elbow on the desk and his chin cupped between thumb and forefinger for several minutes.

'Hmm ... two days' defaulters and one day's pay docked.'

King couldn't believe his ears, and looked to be on the point of exploding. The CO, now with his other elbow on the desk and his chin resting on both of his knuckles so that his chin was jutting forwards, looked at King with an expression that shouted *'just you try to question my ruling.'* 'Carry on Sarg'em.' Not even the customary 'Sergeant Major'.

With a scowl on his face King came to attention.

'Saar. Prisoner hat's on, right turn quick march, left right left right ...'

There was a roar of delight when the Flight heard about the leniency of the sentence handed out to Jack. It was just what was needed to lift their very low spirits. They even had a muted party in the NAAFI that evening to celebrate the snub to King's authority. They'd all liked 'young Dave' and Jack had been considered to be a bloody hero for trying to get him back, even though he'd failed. However, none of them – including Jack – could have guessed how the next part of the saga would very soon unfold.

The next Saturday a handful of the Flight members were in the local; it was not exactly a wake for David, but his name came up in the conversations quite a lot. At about her usual time Eunice King entered the bar. No-one was forthcoming with an offer of a drink, so she made her way to the bar and ordered her usual port and lemon. After about a quarter of an hour when her glass was almost empty, she started to sidle her way towards where Jack was sitting. His first reaction was revulsion; he adjusted his position on the padded bench and was about to move away, when an idea suddenly occurred to him ... He'd spent ages trying to think of some way to make King pay and here it was literally in his lap. She sat down close to him; he turned to her and smiled – that wasn't easy.

'You look very nice tonight, Mrs King.'

The look on the faces of two of Jack's companions had to be seen to be believed – aghast was not quite strong enough to describe it. One of them actually had his mouth wide open.

Both of them slowly slid away and made their way towards the bar, still in a state of shocked disbelief.

'Thank you young man, that's very nice of you.'

'And a bloody lie too,' thought Jack.

'I don't think that I have seen you in here before, have I?' she asked.

'I've been here a few times and seen you, but you've always been the centre of attention.' That wasn't a lie – everyone would have been keeping an eye on her to make sure they didn't become the next victim.

'You're too kind, young man. What's your name?'

'I'm called Jack, Mrs King. I was a friend of the young chap that killed himself.'

'Yes that was very unfortunate,' she said.

Not 'very sad' or 'very upsetting' just 'unfortunate', Jack noted.

'Please call me Eunice, Jack – we don't need to stand on formalities.'

'Can I buy you another drink?' he asked, knowing the answer before it was given.

When he got to the bar he ordered a pint of old and mild and a double port and lemon for Eunice.

'Right, Jack,' said the barmaid, but her eyes said '*what the hell are you up to? She never has double ports*'.

Jack repeated the trip to the bar once more about half an hour later for another double port. He continued plying Eunice with charming comments and she looked like she was really enjoying herself. She also looked increasingly tipsy.

'Would you excuse me for a moment, Eunice,' said Jack when he noticed a fellow recruit near the bar who was well known – well, actually notorious – as a 'ladies man'. It was said he'd shag anything.

'Dennis, have you got any 'johnnies' on you?' whispered Jack. Dennis looked across towards Eunice King and then back to Jack.

'You've got to be joking. Even I wouldn't ...' He was well aware of his own reputation.

'Well? Have you?'

'I always carry a pack of three just in case.'

'Will you sell me one?'

'For that,' he said, nodding towards Eunice, 'you can have one on the house'. Taking care that no-one could see, he took one from a pack and handed it to Jack. 'Do you want me to inform your next of kin?'

Jack gave him a knowing smile and made his way back to where Eunice was sitting, once again with a nearly empty glass. Jack was thinking of the now seriously depleted money in his pocket, but the cost would be well worthwhile.

'I know you said you only have three drinks, but would you like a cherry brandy, Eunice?'

'That's very kind of you Jack. Oh, why not?' Her face was beginning to take on an alcoholic flush and her speech was slurred.

Unbeknown to her she once again she had a double, followed a little later by another. They left the pub at twenty to ten. It was cold, made even colder by that familiar easterly wind. As they came out through the door it felt quite icy. Eunice began visibly to sway.

'Would you like me to accompany to the entrance to the married quarters?' asked Jack.

'You're so considerate, Jack and you don't have to worry luvvy – the MP patrols won't be around until after eleven o'clock, so you can take me further,' she said, nudging him with her elbow.

It would be lights out in the Flight in quarter of an hour – he wasn't going to be there.

When they reached the Kings' house, Eunice unlocked the door, turned and made the too loud and exaggerated 'shush' of a drunk and then beckoned him in. Once inside she mumbled 'the old man won't be 'ome for ages. Give me a minute then come upstairs – I need a pee first.' She then made her way unsteadily up the stairs.

He heard her drag the po from under the bed. There was a lot of splashing that didn't sound as if it was all taking place inside the po. This was followed by some muttering and sounds of furniture being bumped into. Jack waited a long ten minutes: all seemed to be quiet so he made his way up the stairs. When he got to the small landing he could see into the bedroom off to the left – there in the dim light he could make out Eunice sprawled on the bed, legs apart. Alongside her were her dress and cardigan; her knickers were on the floor near the po, which was half under the bed. Her lipstick was all smeared as if she had just wiped it with the back of her hand. She was fast asleep with her mouth wide open snoring. She looked her age.

Jack took the French letter out of his pocket, stretched it, then blew into it so that it was fully extended. Then he crumpled it up and dropped it into the po, which was surrounded by a small puddle. He edged round the bed to the other side and ruffled the bedding, to make it look as if someone else had been in the bed. From his pocket he took what he wanted to be a poignant reminder to King and stuffed it under the pillow on that side. After edging carefully round the bed, again making sure to avoid the puddle, he walked over to the door and without closing it behind him, made his way down the stairs.

He was just about to open the front door when he heard a key being inserted on the other side. It could only be one person. 'The devil incarnate' as far as Jack was concerned. Sergeant Major King was home and for some unexplained reason he was early.

Throwing caution to the wind, in the unknown layout of his surroundings and in almost total darkness, Jack ran as quickly and as quietly as he could towards the back of the house. Fortune favoured the brave. He ran into an open room which turned out to be the kitchen, without bumping into anything. King was also making his way to the kitchen when he was distracted by Eunice calling out in a slurred voice

'Where are you, luvvy?'

At the moment King walked into the bedroom, Jack slipped out of the front door. As he made his escape, listening intently for the MP patrol, he couldn't help hearing a very one-sided shouting match coming from the bedroom. The shouting had attracted the patrol, and Jack heard them coming at the double. By lying flat behind a row of dustbins he was able to hide as the two MPs ran past, towards the house.

When he slipped into the Flight, Jack was surprised to discover that it was not yet eleven o'clock. Now it was a case of getting into bed, having a sleep, and then waiting for the morning or until 'the shit hit the fan', which – of course – it did.

✤

Eunice was seen by one of the girls who worked in the NAAFI. As she was getting off the bus from Ramsgate, she spotted Eunice on the other side of the road, getting on the bus to Ramsgate with two cases, and nursing what looked like a black eye. By breakfast time, word had got around the camp and everyone was warned to avoid King at all costs because he was in the mother and father of bad moods. This of course was linked to the rumour that Jack had shagged Eunice and King had sent her packing. When someone in Jack's group asked him directly, 'come on Jack, did you really shag Eunice?' he kept the rumour alive by replying in an affected voice:

'Gentlemen do not tell about such things'.

The rumour that evening became the only talking point when it was learned that Corporal Rydal had been ordered to escort Aircraftsman Toulson to the CO's office, where Sergeant Major King was to lay serious offence charges against Jack.

'Even if it means a spell in Aldershot Military Prison it will be well worth it,' thought Jack. It was to be exactly that, but not in a way that he could even have imagined. As soon as the usual ritual 'prisoner and escort left right left right left right, prisoner and escort right turn, prisoner hats off' etc had been observed, the CO looked directly at Jack.

'Sergeant Major King has laid some extremely serious charges against you, Toulson,' he said. 'You are charged with trespass within the Married Quarters area, and entering one of the dwellings, namely the residence of Sergeant Major King, during the hours of darkness with the intent of committing a felony. This is contrary to very specific and detailed regulations. The offence having taken place between the hours of 22:00 hours and 23:00 hours last night. What have you to say about these charges, Aircraftsman Toulson?'

'Not guilty, sir. I escorted Mrs King from the Rose and Crown to the Married Quarters entrance because she seemed to be a little inebriated and unsteady on her feet, but I left her at the gate so that I could get to my Flight before lights out.'

Jack could actually feel King seething with anger alongside him.

'One minute, Toulson. Corporal, are you in charge of Aircraftsman's Toulson's Flight?'

'Yes sir,' said Rydal.

'Was he in the Flight by lights out?'

There was a pause. *This is it,* thought Jack.

'Yes, sir,' said Rydal.

King visibly stiffened, his nostrils flared and his already crimson face took on a deeper hue. *'Mistake, Rydal,'* thought King *'I'll have your stripes for that – you're messing with the wrong one, and you don't know the ace that I've got up my sleeve.'*

'Well, Sergeant Major. Toulson doesn't seem to have any case to answer. That is, unless you have any evidence to the contrary. Did anyone see him?'

King braced himself.

'No-one saw him, saar, but I do have evidence. When Toulson was in my house he accidently dropped his personal, and might I add unauthorised, ID bracelet with his service number engraved on it.'

King was not going to say where he had found it. With that, he placed the bracelet on the CO's desk. Corporal Rydal looked decidedly sick, as he visualised his two stripes disappearing. Jack's face showed no emotion. King looked quite triumphant and obviously was enjoying the moment. The CO, who until then had been thinking that the case against Airman Toulson was too flimsy, was beginning to have second thoughts.

'What have you got to say about that, Toulson?' demanded the CO.

'I've no idea, sir. I don't have an ID bracelet.'

'Well, how do you think it has your service number on it?'

'I don't know, sir. Could I have a look at it, sir?'

'Yes, Toulson' said the CO, but there was now quite an icy edge to his tone.

Jack picked up the bracelet and looked at it.

'This is not my number, sir – my service number is 343446 this is 343449. It must have belonged to David White.'

King grabbed the bracelet and looked at it. The CO was obviously taken aback.

'In that case, Sergeant Major, I am going to have to dismiss the charges against Airman Toulson,' he said.

The next fifteen seconds seemed like almost as many minutes, with the events appearing to take place in slow motion. Yet the happenings in that brief instant were life-changing for those in the room. After nearly twenty-five years of disciplined behaviour, King suddenly lost all his self-control. Two decades of festering resentment, which had grown to utter hatred, came to the fore. King swung his fist at Jack, hitting him on his right eye and knocking him to the ground. The CO called the two guards who were standing just outside his office. The now out-of-control Sergeant Major picked up his pace stick, which he had earlier placed on the cabinet alongside the CO's desk, and grabbed at the CO. He missed him because Rydal had moved to intervene. So King swung at the CO with his faithful pace stick; the CO managed to move his head out of the way of the blow, but there was an ominous crack as the stick hit him on the shoulder. Corporal Rydal tried to wrest the stick from King and was punched on the side of the face for his efforts. King was not overcome, until the two guards entered the room.

This was not the outcome that Jack had hoped for: it was better – so much better. King was sentenced to six months in Aldershot Military Prison, was dishonourably discharged, lost his pension – and lost his wife.

※

When he had entered the CO's office, Jack had thought that with a bit of luck he might be able to get away with what he'd done, and in the process put an end to Eunice's tormenting of recruits, and leave King with nagging doubts about his wife. He realised that King would try to make his life hell until he left Manston, but it would have been well worth it. The unexpected outcome, the removal of King – who turned out to be one of the last Sergeant Majors in the RAF – caused a complete change in the character and quality of life on the base.

King was replaced by a non-technical Flight Sergeant who was strict but fair. The number of airmen appearing at defaulters' parade plummeted without any loss of discipline. The CO, who had suffered a broken collar bone, returned to duty six weeks after the event, and Corporal Rydal was promoted to Sergeant before the end of the year. This was a very popular promotion, particularly with Flight C. He and Jack were both considered to be 'bloody heroes.'

After all the activity in the CO's office was over, Jack reflected upon how it had come about. His thoughts kept coming back to that period when he had endured the depths of angry frustration, when he had not arrived in time to save Dave. He recalled when he had cut poor Dave's body down and found the envelope addressed to 'The best of all friends – Jack.'

It was written in indelible pencil and Jack was haunted by the parts where David's tears had fallen on some of the writing and turned it purple.

> **Dearest Friend Jack, I am sorry but I am so afraid of going to Aldershot. I can't face the shame it would bring to my parents so I must take the coward's way out. I would like you to have my ID bracelet to remember me by. Please remember how we started out on the great adventure together; we did have some fun, didn't we? Could you please make sure that my parents receive the page addressed them. Goodbye and good luck, your friend David.**

As Jack read it, his throat had tightened and tears had welled up in his eyes. Dave had become his younger brother. Jack hadn't given the envelope to the police. Perhaps he should have done but he hadn't been able to bring himself to do so. The coroner had ruled that 'Airman David White had taken his own life whilst his balance of mind had been disturbed'. Jack had ruled that an evil bastard had driven him to commit suicide as the only way out.

※

On his next leave, just over a month later, Jack went first to see his family, then on the second day he told them that he had to go to Halifax to sort something out.

'It's for Dave, the one I told thee about, the one who 'ung imself.'

When Jack approached Dave's parents' house in Halifax, he realised how different Dave's family situation was to that of his own. No scrimping and scraping here, in fact no going without at all. It was a big house with a large garden, on a tree-lined avenue. He rang the bell and a maid, complete with a small starched white apron and small starched white hat, answered the door, gave him a small starched gaze and asked him what he wanted. He asked to see Mr and Mrs White.

'I have a letter from David,' he said.

He was shown into the front parlour, where he was not invited to sit down. Mrs White came in first, and immediately Jack could see where 'young Dave' had got his looks; there was no question that this was his mother, but unlike Dave she had fair hair.

'I'm Jack Toulson. I was a friend of your son David' – Jack remembered that his parents always insisted upon him being called David – 'I would like to offer you my condolences on your sad loss.'

Although Mrs White had managed to keep the looks of her younger years extremely well, her recent grief had wreaked havoc on her face, her eyes were red-rimmed with dark shadows around them, but her underlying beauty shone through all of that.

'Thank you, Jack,' she said. 'It's very kind of you to take the trouble to come to see us.'

Jack could hear and sense the control that Mrs White had to exert in order to make sure her voice didn't break. She was very close to tears.

'Mr White will be joining us very soon.'

As if on cue, Mr White entered the room. Jack couldn't see any of Dave's features in his father, who also had fair hair like his wife.

'Well, young man, who are you?'

'I'm Jack Toulson.'

'He was a friend of David,' said Mrs White.

Jack could see that she was anxious to be part of the conversation, because here was a connection with her beloved David, someone who could tell her all about her son's life in the RAF.

'Oh yes, I recall him mentioning you,' said Mr White.

'Lancelot! David talked about Jack all the time when he was on leave,' she interrupted, with more than a hint of annoyance in her voice.

'That's as maybe, Letitia. May we offer you a cup of tea, young man? Ring for Alice, Letitia.'

87

'Thank you sir,' said Jack, 'but I really came to give you a letter that David left with me.' He offered the letter to Mrs White, but Mr White took it.

'Wasn't it in an envelope?' he asked.

'I'm afraid not, sir,' lied Jack. 'That's how David gave it to me.'

Mr White took the sheet, which had been folded in four. On the outside was written 'Mr and Mrs White (Father and Mama)'. He opened it.

> **Life has become just too unbearable. I have managed to get myself into trouble again, and, it is most likely that I will end up causing you a great deal of shame and embarrassment among your friends and neighbours. Please forgive me, your loving son David.**

After a couple of brief seconds, Mr White folded the piece of paper again, put the letter in his pocket and turned to his wife:

'I think it would be better if you read this later, my dear, when our guest has gone,' he said.

It wasn't a suggestion, but an instruction. He looked irritated rather than upset. He tapped the piece of paper and said to Jack: 'I see his handwriting never did improve. Just like his mother – see this thing that looks like the letter "b"? It's supposed to be a capital "L".'

Jack was so astonished that Mr White, reading the suicide note of his only son, would comment on such a trivial thing as his handwriting, that he said nothing.

Eventually, Mr White spoke again.

'How did David manage to get himself into trouble again, young man?'

The blunt question directed at Jack was a difficult one to answer.

'Well, sir, David had managed to upset the Sergeant Major, who was being rather harsh with him, and he was taking action that would result in a bad report being placed on David's service record. David had so wanted to keep his record clean, to please you, and you, ma'am.'

'But he did upset the Sergeant Major, after I had told him to try to get into his good books,' the father muttered, shaking his head.

'David did try, sir.'

'Obviously he did not try hard enough, young man.'

'The Sergeant Major had been very severe with David, sir, and soon after David died, he had a breakdown and was dismissed from the RAF.'

'Poor man must have felt responsible in some way, just for doing his duty.'

*'Poor man my arse, that bastard **was** responsible, and he got just what he deserved'*. This was what Jack wanted to say, but he managed to hold his tongue.

Ignoring a warning look from her husband, Mrs White said: 'the RAF sent David's personal belongings to us. We particularly cherish the ID bracelet that we gave him as a Christmas present. It's such a pity that his name couldn't have been engraved on it. It seems so sad to be remembered just by a number. Of course my husband knows about these things, even though he has never been in the armed services. It was fortunate that he did, otherwise David would not have been able to wear it if we had had his name engraved on it.'

'No, that would have been sad,' said Jack. '*What a load of old bollocks,*' he thought. This confirmed the impression that he had formed of Dave's father, although he did agree that it was fortunate that Dave's name had not been engraved on the ID bracelet. He didn't mention that Dave had wanted him to have it.

'I expect that you have brothers and sisters, young man,' said Mr White 'David is ... was our only child – unfortunately his mother was unable to have more children, so he will be sorely missed.'

'I am sure that he will, sir. David and me were good friends and I know that I will miss him.' '*Sorely missed? Is that all?*' Jack thought.

Soon after that, the maid brought in the tea, which was served in fine bone-china cups, together with fairy cakes on a stand with fine bone-china plates to place them on. Jack was able to give Mrs White a lengthy detailed account of Dave's short career in the RAF, albeit a carefully edited version. He saw her face brighten when he truthfully told her how all of the members of Flight C had liked him, and had always tried to help him when he had to sort out his kit.

'He had a lot of friends, ma'am.'

'I'm pleased to hear that, Jack. He never had many friends when he was at school,' she said in a quiet voice, and looked accusingly at her husband. A look that said *'and we all know whose fault that was.'*

It was dark when Jack left. He was pleased that he had delivered the letter, but he knew that Dave's mother would, without doubt, break down when she read it. It was only as he was walking back to the railway station that he realised Dave had never mentioned that he didn't have any brothers or sisters. Although he had been impressed by what they owned and how rich they were with all of their possessions, he realised how poor they were in family affections. No wonder Dave had been so anxious to make friends.

That evening when the family were sitting in the scullery, Jack fascinated them all with descriptions of how the visit to Halifax had gone. They all hung on his every word when he described how the wealthy people lived. Then he told them how he became aware that, for all their possessions, their lives were not as rich as people like the Toulson family.

'They don't behave like a real family – everything seems to be a pretence and show for the benefit of the neighbours,' he said.

At this, he saw the Old Man smile at Mother.

The short leave was a very happy time with the family, and this went some way to make up for the very bad preceding two months.

❧

Back at Manston, the training proceeded at quite a pace. When they enlisted, the recruits had been classified as 'carpenters' but by the end of the course they were reclassified as 'carpenter riggers'.

Jack often thought about Dave and how he would have enjoyed life in the RAF. It was definitely not as his father had described, but nevertheless it was still a great adventure. For some while Jack managed to keep in touch with Esme and George and visited them every few months when he was able to get a 72-hour pass. Esme gave birth to a little boy a week after the anniversary of Dave's death. They named him Brian.

Two days after Brian's first birthday, Jack went to visit George and Esme and their children. It was a rather sad visit because Jack and his fellow recruits had now finished training. It had been a very mixed eighteen months with some very dark lows and a few occasional bright highs, but all in all it had been a period of increased self awareness and character building for Jack and his surviving fellow Flight members.

The week after his visit to his friends in Blean he was posted to another RAF station. In fact he was not to see George and his family again until Mary was eight years old.

CHAPTER TEN

For the next eight moons the routine with the Queen of Sheba's party took on a regular pattern. Although the Queen enjoyed the show of wealth with the pool in the reception hall, she asked Solomon to have stepping stones placed in the water so that the door at the front of the palace could be accessed more easily.

Each and every day the Queen would be taken to have an audience with Solomon and would put to him what seemed like endless difficult questions. And every day the Queen would be astounded by the wisdom of his answers. Following the first new moon after their arrival, the Queen announced to her retinue that they would no longer be following a morning ritual of worshipping the Sun. Instead they would worship a God about whom King Solomon had been instructing her. This disconcerted some of her followers and they were quite fearful of what might befall them if they failed to continue with their worship – a handful of them until the next new moon secretly continued the practice but after they saw that nothing dreadful happened to the rest of their companions they also discontinued worshipping the Sun God.

Between the fifth and sixth new moons, quite late one afternoon, Solomon and the Queen were talking about valuable woods.

'The most precious wood, of course, is from the juniper tree,' said the Queen. Among the gifts that she had presented to Solomon were five camel-loads of juniper wood.

King Solomon looked very contemplative, and then he said in an almost conspiratorial voice – as if he was about to divulge a forbidden secret: 'Tomorrow I will show you a wood far more precious than all others.'

The Queen was intrigued.

The next day, Solomon told her that the commander of her bodyguards could accompany her and he would have one of his aides to accompany him. As soon as the rest of the court had been dismissed, Solomon, the Queen of Sheba, Fariq and Kariz made their way to the middle of the palace. In the side of one of the corridors there was a small concealed door. Fariq and Kariz were told to stand guard outside the door. Solomon unlocked it with a key that was hung on a gold chain around his neck. He indicated for the Queen of Sheba to step inside and he followed her, locking the door behind them. The only light in the room was from a minute barred opening in the ceiling, which in turn was illuminated by light from another room above. Solomon then walked to the corner that was to the right of the door and pushed on the wall. Part of it moved to reveal a cupboard about three cubits tall and half a cubit wide. He reached inside and reverently took from the cupboard a rod which was about two cubits in length, and not much wider than his thumb. He then carefully handed it to the Queen.

'Surely this is not valuable? It is no special wood – what on Earth could you use it for?'

Solomon smiled – in a rather fatherly way.

'When you were lost in the desert what did you think was the most precious thing in creation?'

The Queen paused and gave the question some thought – her talks with Solomon had changed the way that she now considered questions. It was noticeable that he didn't interrupt her when she was speaking. She looked directly at him and answered firmly 'water'.

Solomon smiled again and said: 'This is the rod of the leader whom God chose to take his people out of Egypt. If you hold it and pray to the God that I have told you about – and listen – he will speak to you through your inner voice. It will direct your feet and tell you where to strike the ground with the rod. When you strike the ground, then water will gush forth. This rod has been passed down to me through many, many generations. You may have been surprised by the numerous wells and places where water flows in Jerusalem. This has been done secretly by God acting through me, in the same way that he did with his other chosen leader.'

The rod was then carefully replaced in the hidden cupboard and the door to the room was unlocked by Solomon. He and the Queen went out into the corridor. He carefully locked the door, and they all returned to the throne room where Solomon and the Queen held their daily discussions.

The audiences continued until a further two moons had passed, but now the emphasis in the meetings changed.

From the very first meeting Solomon had, in truth, only one objective –and that was to possess this beautiful woman. It was a case of lust at first sight. More of their meetings involved them being taken around Jerusalem in one of Solomon's golden carriages on the pretence of him showing her sights of the city; actually it was really a case of the King showing the Queen of Sheba in his company, as if she was a trophy about to be won. The Queen was without doubt impressed even to a state of awe by what she saw. It was so much larger and more verdant than her town of Marib, which before this visit she had considered to be the greatest oasis-like place in the desert of her homeland.

The time that they spent talking in the palace more or less revolved around King Solomon pointing out that they were both very wealthy rulers and together they could form an even greater Kingdom.

The Queen of Sheba had been crowned during her sixteenth summer. Her mother, who had ruled before her, died from an illness shortly after returning from Ophir. During the Queen's eleven summers on the throne she had become accustomed to various princes and wealthy powerful men attempting to woo her. However none of them had held any attraction for her – and neither did Solomon. Although she greatly admired his wisdom, she had no wish to enter into any carnal relationship with him.

The last part of the visit became increasingly fraught with problems as the Queen spent much of the time, when she was in his company, trying to fend off his attempts to get her to agree to becoming his bride. When the Queen announced her intention to return to Sheba, Solomon said, in a desperate last throw of the dice: 'I will give you the rod of the leader of God's people for you to take to your homeland, if you will solemnly swear that you will not use it before you reach your destination. If you do, you will return here and become my queen.'

The Queen, in order to bring Solomon's pestering to an end, duly swore a solemn oath. This was just two days before she set off with her retinue back to Sheba.

On the night before the departure, one of the Queen's handmaids was paying a farewell visit to a lady who worked in King Solomon's palace and with whom she had become very friendly. It was late in the evening when the friend was called away, leaving the handmaid alone in one of the ante-rooms. She was about to make her way back to the Queen's facility when she slipped on one of the steps of the marble floor and ended up in a narrow space behind one of the statue plinths near the entrance. She was in some pain and one of her ankles was already beginning to swell. She was in the process of extricating herself from where she had become jammed when she heard the unmistakable voice of the King as he approached the door of the ante-room. She immediately and instinctively stopped trying to get up and moved further behind the plinth – better to keep out of sight when his majesty was around.

He came in with one of his soldiers.

'Check that there is no-one in the corridor, Fariq.'

The command was immediately obeyed.

'The corridor is completely empty, your majesty.'

'I have a very important mission for you, probably the most important mission that you will ever have to carry out -'

'Yes your maje ...'

'- in your life. This is to be most secret. No-one is to hear even a whisper about it – '

'No your ma ...'

'- under pain of death you understand. And stop interrupting me.'

Fariq just managed to stop himself from saying anything. Solomon was showing his human trait of not being able to tolerate his own failings in others.

'Tomorrow the Queen of Sheba with her caravan will be leaving for her homeland. I want you to select ten of your best men and follow them unobserved. You are to take with you two camels loaded with salt.'

Fariq was about to say 'salt?' but he kept silent.

'On the night after the eighth day after the caravan has left Hegra, I want you and your men to enter the caravan camp secretly and put salt in all of the water carriers except the top layer on each camel. Then for the next fifteen days I want you to continue following the caravan, remaining unseen to observe what happens. You are to take particular care to watch the Queen, especially if she leaves the caravan on her own or with only a few of her retinue. After that you are to return and report back.'

There was a long pause. Fariq didn't know whether to speak or not.

'Well?'

'Yes, your majesty.'

'Go and make your preparations then,' said the King tetchily, adding in a more threatening tone, 'and don't fail me.'

The commander left, but he was not quite sure what failure entailed. The King was obviously not in a good mood.

The handmaid remained out of sight until at long last the King left the ante-room and made his way to the main chambers. Her ankle by now didn't look very good at all. However with a few muted winces and gritting of teeth she managed to extract herself from where she had been trapped. Quickly and quietly she limped her way back to the Queen's apartments. Once there she had her ankle massaged with soothing oils and wrapped with small pieces of cloth by one of her colleagues. Then she reported for her normal duties.

'What have you done to your foot?' asked the Queen when she noticed that her handmaid was limping. The handmaid proceeded to tell of how she had become trapped behind one of the statues in the ante-room of King Solomon's palace. After she had asked the Queen if she could speak in private and the other handmaids had been asked to wait in their room, she went on to tell the Queen what she had overheard about Solomon's plans. The Queen immediately sent word for her chief advisor, Kariz, and Zeki to attend her. As soon as they were all assembled, the handmaid was asked to repeat what she had overheard. Although she was very nervous, she did so as calmly as she could manage. After she had completed her account she was complimented for bringing the matter to the Queen's attention, instructed not to say anything about it to anyone else, and then sent

to rejoin her colleagues. The meeting of the Queen and the senior members of her cortege lasted for some while. Plans were made.

The next morning, one of Solomon's officials came to the Queen's palace to invite her, for the last time, to an audience with the King. As on the previous occasion, when Solomon had shown her the rod of Moses, the King – accompanied by Fariq – and the Queen – with Kariz by her side – made their way to the hidden chamber. Solomon and the Queen of Sheba went inside; Solomon took the rod from its place of safekeeping, wrapped it in thick parchment and with his royal insignia sealed it with wax in three places. He handed it to the Queen saying 'Guard it well. And remember your solemn oath.' After this they returned to the anteroom where the audience was concluded with a protracted farewell ceremony.

The Queen, with her small retinue, returned to her soon-to-be-evacuated palace. Outside the residence the camels of the caravan were being loaded and preparations for the journey were almost complete. Shahin – the bodyguard with vision like an eagle – was at the rear of the caravan and appeared to be helping with the loading, but in reality most of his time was spent in scrutinising the onlookers. The crowd appeared to be of the usual type that always seemed to gather whenever a caravan was about to leave. After about ten minutes he wiped his forehead and put the part of his turban that was hanging down on his chest over his left shoulder. This was a pre-arranged signal to let the commander know that they were being watched by at least one of Solomon's men on the left of the caravan. Zeki, with two of his men, went to the back of the caravan and made a show about securing all the water supplies on the last four camels and telling the men in charge of them how important the water was. With that, Zeki and his men moved to the front. The Queen was escorted out of the palace for the final time and joined the caravan. The senior advisor gave the signal and the caravan moved off, bound for Sheba.

Hegra came and went, and sure enough, eight nights later the guards saw and heard Fariq with his men when they crept into the caravan camp. The intruders were dressed as outlaws, not as soldiers. They made their way to where the camels were bedded down and the water-filled skins were stacked.

'There should be twenty-four of them,' whispered Fariq to one

of his men. 'Make sure they are filled with water and then add the salt, but not to the skins that they will use during the next five days.'

The whispered order was passed on and then carried out. When the task was completed, the intruders quietly – by their standards – left the camp the same way that they had entered.

When they were about a thousand paces from the encampment, Fariq – who was feeling quite pleased with himself – congratulated his men on their efficient completion of the first part of the mission.

The next morning Kariz and Zeki called their men together for one of the joint meetings that were becoming more and more of a feature of the day-to-day procedures in the caravan.

'Well that was a shambles – certainly not the way to conduct a covert operation,' said Kariz. Everyone nodded agreement. Zeki was involving his men more and more in the training and practice procedures that the Queen's bodyguards used.

'They were too spread out,' he said. 'They should have approached by lying much flatter, and there should have been far fewer exchanges of commands.'

It was Kariz's turn to nod in agreement.

For the next fifteen days as the caravan continued south, Shahin – without difficulty – watched Fariq and his men as they strained their eyes peering to keep watch on the caravan. They were completely mistaken in the belief that they were out of sight. After a further two days Shahin reported to Kariz that they were no longer being followed.

❦

The day after the caravan left Jerusalem, Solomon summoned his newly appointed envoy for the south.

'You are to go to Marib,' he ordered. 'Make sure you arrive before the Queen of Sheba's caravan. When she arrives you are to immediately present yourself and ask ... no, demand ... to see the package sealed by King Solomon. Make sure that you examine it very carefully. As the seal will be broken you have to tell the Queen that she has to return to Jerusalem because of her solemn oath. You are then to return with her.'

This new envoy had been warned not to interrupt the King, so he waited until he was very sure that the King had finished speaking.

'What if the seal is not broken, your majesty?'

King Solomon smiled wryly. 'It will be.'

The dismissed envoy hurried away to perform his first official task. He left at sunrise the following morning with a small contingent of soldiers and assistants. With such a small camel train it would be very easy to overtake the large caravan of the Queen of Sheba, which they did just before the next full moon, not long after they passed Fariq and his men returning to Jerusalem.

CHAPTER ELEVEN

When the postings came out, the 'old' Flight C was split up and dispersed to various aerodromes in the UK: the quartet of Jack, Gus, Clive, and Ginger ended up at Henlow. This was a bit too far for Jack to visit Blean, but he did keep in touch. He sent letters and sometimes cards to both young Mary and Brian on their birthdays.

The quartet spent almost two years at Henlow, working on many different types of aircraft. All four of them during their time there became reclassified as ACIs (Aircraftsmen first class), and in the April of 1923 they all were posted to the RAF Depot Egypt, near Cairo, where Squadron 47 was based.

As the Vickers Vernon with almost two dozen airmen packed in it came into land at the airbase, completing the last leg of the flight from Hendon, Jack recalled Dave's enthusiastic descriptions on the train of Wing Commander Bowhill's escapades in Somaliland. Was it really four years ago? It would not be long before the new arrivals in the 'dark continent' would become witnesses of acts of more derring-do themselves. How Dave would have enjoyed this posting!

As they started clambering down the short ladder to the ground, Clive – who was the first to disembark – called out 'who the bloody hell said this was the 'dark continent'? The sun's so bleeding bright it effing well nearly blinds you, and it's hot enough to fry your nackers.' Everyone in the disembarking contingent agreed with his assessment as they set foot on the dusty runway. No nice, firm, comforting tarmac runways here – tarmac would have melted.

The quartet were about to experience a dramatic change in their duties. During the two years they had been stationed at Henlow, they had only attended three crash sites between them. Within a week of arriving in Egypt, each of them had attended a 'recovery and retrieval' operation which involved a crash, and all of these had been within twenty miles of the airfield. Deployment on 'recovery and retrieval' was to become something they would experience with a frequency and regularity that was never monotonous and often tragic. Sometimes it was possible to retrieve material and parts for use in the repair of other damaged aircraft, but more often than not the operation would just end up with the burning of the remains of the crashed plane.

As they were close to Cairo, when they were granted 'passes' they were permitted to go off base, but they always had to be back on base by 23:59 hours. No-one was allowed to sleep off the base. This meant that they were able to visit many of the antiquity sites, including the pyramids, which was something that most of the people back home only read about in books.

Soon after their arrival at the depot the 'newly arrived' were given a lecture, complete with a graphic slide show, about the dangers of venereal disease, and were warned to keep away from the local brothels. To reinforce this they were told that there would be a fortnightly FFI (freedom from infection) inspection. Despite all the warnings, two months later – Clive who had acquired a bit of a reputation for being a randy bugger – failed an FFI inspection and was carted off to hospital. After he returned to the camp he regaled his mates with lurid tales of his treatment:

'Well there I was, laid on me bed, and in comes the MO. He takes out this bloody great syringe, jabs it up the eye of me todger and then he spends quarter of an hour rinsing in and out me poor old knob with some stuff that looked like and smelt like 'Pusser's purple'. I don't mind telling you, it fair put me teeth on edge and brought tears to me eyes. After he'd taken the syringe out, he replaced it with a small rubber tube connected to a bottle of the Pusser's purple, and it was 'ung above me bed for hours on end. After a week they stopped putting the tube in but the next day me balls became all red and swollen – they told me that I now had epy- dimy- ditis, they reckoned that it 'appens to everyone who 'as the tube treatment, but it meant another three days in the 'ospital. I'll tell you what – me balls still feel a bit sore.'

'Serves you right Clive,' said Jack. 'We were warned, and blimey mate, the local bints have got faces that would turn milk sour.'

'You're a fine one to talk, Jack – the bloke who shagged Eunice.'

Although it had been four years now, and Jack had denied more times than he could remember that he'd 'had it away' with Eunice, he was still stuck with the label, and in a way it made him a bit of a folk hero. The cheerful banter went on for quite some while.

Clive was still having some discomfort with his scrotum a week later when he was posted to somewhere in 'the British Mandate of Mesopotamia' where there was a war going on. Clive's escapades and description of what had happened to him proved to be a far more effective deterrent than any of the talks and slide shows put on by the MO.

It was a year before the remaining trio was posted to Abu Qir (Aboukir) Aircraft depot, where they remained for six months until it was their turn to get a posting to a war zone. All three were sent to a region where there were hostilities taking place, although people back home in Blighty knew nothing about it. They were posted to RAF Aden.

The journey from Abu Qir to Aden was quite a treat and an adventure for the trio. During the journey, once again Jack couldn't help thinking how much this would have meant to young Dave. A group of just over two dozen of them was transported to Port Said by lorry where they embarked on a P&O ship, which was on its way to India. It took them down the Suez Canal and through the Red Sea to Steamer point at Aden. The voyage took just seven days and the trio thoroughly enjoyed it. After disembarking, they were transported from the port in Crater to the airbase at Khor Maksar, which was to be their home for the next two-and-a-half years. The base had the motto 'into the remote places' – and for good reason. Although it was only six or seven miles from the town and was on the isthmus that joined Aden to the mainland, it did seem a lot more remote.

They were about exchange a hot climate for a hotter one, but on the day that they arrived there was a torrential downpour that flooded parts of the camp near the canvas-and-timber Bessonneau hangars which had been used in France during the Great War. Through the open front of one of them they could see some DH 9ACs, affectionately known as 'Ninacks', which had become one of their favourite aircraft frames to work on during their spell at Cairo. According to the driver of the lorry that brought them and their kitbags from the port, this was the first rain that had been seen for nearly six months. The resultant flooding disappeared just as quickly as it had appeared.

Jack, Ginger and Gus were now effectively deployed to an 'unknown war'. Even those on the airbase, perhaps with the exception of the Commanding Officer and a few of his senior personnel, had no idea about what was going on. They were told there were some tribesmen who were trying to take over land which would be contrary to the interests of 'Britannia', and it was the 'given duty' of the RAF to support those tribesmen who were trying to prevent this happening.

At the beginning of the third week after the new contingent arrived at Khor Maksar, some were engaged in the first of what was soon to become regular 'recovery and retrieval' operations similar to those that the trio had grown accustomed to in Cairo. The only difference here was that the recovery teams, accompanied by army personnel, had to travel greater distances.

The camp at Khor Maksar, despite its motto, maintained the character and discipline of any RAF base. The roadways within the perimeter were lined with whitewashed rocks. The entrance to the camp was on the south side of the airfield, and looking south from the camp entrance the jagged peaks surrounding Crater dominated the skyline and created the impression of a barrier between the base and the outside world, adding to the sense of isolation. The view looking north from the northern perimeter of the airfield didn't help; there was what appeared to be just a great expanse of desert. Getting to Crater from the RAF camp was not easy: although it was only a similar distance to that from Manston to Ramsgate, here there was no bus service and the journey could only be undertaken when RAF transport was available. Needless to say, trips into Aden after the initial novelty had worn off became few and far between.

A very welcome change to the dress code was the issue of tropical gear. The RAF blue serge was replaced with sandy-coloured knee-length shorts and short-sleeved shirts. The headgear was changed to sandy-coloured pith helmets. Throughout their complete tour of duty at Aden, the trio rarely saw the daytime temperature fall below 85° F.

Although just beyond the eastern boundary of the camp was a long flat wide area of beach that bounded the Indian Ocean, surprisingly swimming was not a particularly popular activity despite the high temperatures.

To celebrate the anniversary of their arrival in Aden, the trio had a bit of a party in the evening with a few others who had been posted with them from Abu Qir.

'Don't seem like a year since we came 'ere, does it, Jack?'

'You're right there, Ginge. It ain't been too bad, but sometimes I get the feeling that they've forgotten all about us. I don't think we'll be going 'ome for some while yet.'

'I 'ope you two ain't getting maudlin,' said Gus, looking a little bleary eyed over the half full glass in front of him.

Together with most of the airmen on the base, they were beginning to have the impression that not much was changing in the war that was going on between the various tribesmen.

The following morning, Gus and Jack were working on an aircraft in one of the hangars. They had heard a couple of planes land, but they hadn't taken much notice – it was nothing out of the ordinary. Ginger ran into the hangar.

'Hey you two – I want you to come and meet an old friend of ours,' he said.

They went over to the runway. Two Vickers Vernons were parked there. Although none of them had remembered the number on the plane that had carried them from Hendon to Cairo, they all remembered the name on its bulbous nose, and here it was again for all to see -'Adam', their old winged chariot. The other proudly carried the name 'Eve' emblazoned on its unmistakeable schnozzle. When they had been transported in it, there had been nearly two dozen of them packed in as passengers. But in this case there were less than a dozen in each aircraft. This was because these passengers were high-ranking government officials with their ladies. There was a rumour about a meeting to be held at the Political Resident's offices between the tribal leaders who were fighting for Britannia's interest, and important British officials.

This rumour appeared to have some substance to it because within a month the tempo of activity on the base increased quite dramatically, the number of bombing raids that were carried out almost quadrupled, and the number of recovery operations consequently increased, as did the distances travelled to make the recoveries. The invading tribesmen were at last being driven back.

Gus was part of one team that went to a site near a village called Yarim. The pilot and the bomber had both been killed in that crash. He was also part of the next recovery exercise, which took place even further north at a place called Dhaner. In this case both occupants of the aircraft survived and useful parts were recovered. Both these recovery operations were plain sailing.

The following week it was Jack's turn to be involved in one of these long-range sorties, but this time it was not quite such a straightforward expedition: the site was even further north, just to the south of the village of Marib, where there had been extensive incursion in the area by the opposing tribesmen. If it hadn't been for the bombing attacks carried out by the RAF, the local pro-British forces would have been overcome.

When the recovery team – together with an Aden Troop contingent – arrived, invading tribesmen were still in the area. Jack had just clambered out of the truck with two other members of the team when suddenly there was a loud crack. A bullet whacked into the sand not five feet from where they were standing! Immediately, all three threw themselves flat on the ground. The half dozen or so of the Aden Troop, there to act as their defence team, sprang into action in an obviously well-practised procedure. The corporal in charge immediately established a defensive perimeter, the recovery team rolled into the relative safety of a dip in the sand between two hummocks, and it seemed almost instantaneously that they heard the Hotchkiss gun barking in short bursts of automatic fire. The remnants of the invading force were no match for this. Within as many minutes, ten of them were either dead or would make acquaintance with their maker before the hour was out.

While Jack and his two colleagues were huddled between the dunes, George's words on the train, a lifetime ago, rang through his head: *'Fighting ain't fun at all, not when all them bullets and shells is whizzing round and you're not sure if the next one's got your name on it.'* Jack now knew exactly what George meant.

The three airmen all felt relieved when the shooting stopped, but the Aden troop appeared to be completely unmoved by the skirmish. Ranjit, the Corporal of the troop, went up to the Sergeant in charge of the RAF personnel and said 'All clear, sahib. I have secured the perimeter around the crash site.'

With that he turned and rejoined the soldier on the Hotchkiss gun, took out his binoculars and proceeded to scan the surrounding area in minute detail.

Jack was surprised that no attempt was made to bury the dead insurgents. Later he found out that the Corporal had lost one of the members of his platoon a month earlier for attempting to do just that. So now he let the carrion take over – the vultures just seemed to appear out of nowhere.

Following the Sergeant's instruction, Jack and the rest of the team set about sorting out the pieces of equipment that were to be removed and taken back to Khor Maksar. Sergeant Taylor was particularly pleased when he discovered that the engine exhaust pipe system was completely intact. Because of a recent flurry in the number of aircraft crashes, stores were running out of certain parts and there was a particular shortage of engine exhaust systems. Finding one in good order was a real bonus.

Jack had recently taken up photography and had bought

a Kodak Hawk-Eye camera from one of the NCOs who had moved on to a new hobby. This was the first time Jack had taken what was to become his 'faithful camera' on a recovery operation, and his first active service picture was the one he took of the Sergeant in front of the downed aircraft, holding up the exhaust pipe system as if it was a hunting trophy. After this Jack was detailed to go and dig a latrine pit. The team took it in turn for this task and today it was his turn.

'There's quite a bit of useful salvage that we can get off this one so we will be here for a couple of days,' said the Sergeant. 'So dig it nice and deep, Jack.'

Most of the NCOs and officers used Christian names when talking to other ranks on these deployment exercises. Jack went to the truck to get a shovel and his water bottle. He had learned that it was important to drink plenty of water when you were out in the desert sun for any length of time. As he was getting out of the truck, he looked in the opposite direction from which the previous assault had been launched. A hundred yards to the north of the vehicle, just outside the defensive perimeter, he could see the remains of what at one time must have been a dwelling place. Jack decided that it would be a good place for the latrine.

The instant he stepped through the gap where at one time there may have been a door to deny entrance, he realised that he'd made a mistake. There could have easily have been one of the invading tribesmen hiding in there. He was just in the act of stepping back from the opening when Ranjit put a hand on his shoulder. Jack hadn't heard him run up.

'Bloody hell! You nearly gave me a heart attack,' he said.

When the Corporal of the Troop had seen Jack going towards the ruin, he had sprinted towards him but had not reached the doorway in time.

'Sorry, sahib, but it was not a good idea to come in here,' he said. 'Let me check it.'

'No, you're right. Thanks. I just thought that it would make a good site for the latrine – I forgot it was outside the 'safe perimeter'.'

'OK, sahib, I will extend the perimeter on this side then it will be fine.'

The Corporal made his way over to one of his men and gave some instructions. Four of his men then changed their positions. After this had been completed, Jack went inside the ruin. He had a good look round and decided that the side in the shade would be the best place to make his excavations. Apart from the shade, the remains of the wall would also afford some privacy. There was a shrub growing in the corner, so he decided dig the 'shit pit', as it was usually called, midway along that wall.

As Jack was about to start digging he remembered the first occasion that he had gone grave digging with his dad, when he was only twelve years old. He smiled as he recalled how his Old Man had told him of something that had happened on a slightly foggy October morning about a week earlier. He'd had to dig a grave next to the railings on the west boundary of the cemetery. He'd started at about half past four in the morning and had nearly finished when he'd realised he'd forgotten to bring with him his much-treasured pocket watch. It had been just beginning to get light, so it would be soon time to make his way back home so that he could get to the steelworks in time. Arriving late was not tolerated if you wanted to keep your job, as everyone did. Those had been hard times. He'd been finishing off at the bottom of the grave when he'd heard the sound of approaching footsteps, the clop, clop of wooden clogs on the cobblestones. It had obviously been one of the workers making his way to the steelworks. As the footsteps had drawn level with the newly dug grave he'd hauled himself up out of the hole and called out 'Does tha 'ave time, lad?'

There had been an anguished yelp as the passerby stopped, looked at the figure crawling out of the grave, and then had run off down the hill. The clop, clop noise of the clogs had been much faster than when it was approaching, and soon had been lost in the early morning gloom.

'I guess he must have thought I was t' grim reaper coming for 'im,' said Jack's dad with a smile on his face.

Jack started to dig the hole, but on the second jab of the shovel he hit wood. *'Well it can't be floorboards, the houses only have mud or stone floors,'* he thought, so he scraped the soil off the wood and it became apparent that it was the top of a box.

He dug all around it and lifted it out of the hole he'd now made. It was about four feet long and about eight inches wide and eight inches deep. Maybe someone had buried a rifle or a large sword? Maybe it was buried treasure? He levered off the top of the box with the edge of the shovel. He decided that he had made enough mistakes for one day so he didn't put his hand into the box to find out what treasure was hidden in it. *'Probably crawling with snakes or scorpions,'* he thought, remembering how every morning it was standard practice to check boots and socks before putting them on, to make sure that there were no venomous temporary lodgers hiding in them, having a siesta.

He took out a match and lit it so he could see what the box contained. No snakes or unpleasant creepy-crawlies and disappointingly no precious stones reflecting their presence back at him, no gold coins, not even a sword or a gun. The only thing in the box was an old stick that had what looked like Arabic writing carved on it. There were a few bits of yellowed paper stuck to the stick and a square piece of wax with some sort of imprint on it, half attached to one of the pieces of paper. Jack carefully pulled the stick from the box, gave it a cursory inspection, threw it to one side, then continued with digging the latrine. When it was finished he walked back to one of the three trucks, threw the shovel and stick in the back, and then made his way to where the team were working on the crashed Ninack.

'The latrine's finished, Sarge. It's in that ruined building over there,' he said, pointing to where he had nearly had kittens.

While Jack had been digging the pit and 'treasure hunting', Sergeant Taylor had had a good look at the poor old kite and had decided that his first impression was quite correct and there was quite a bit of salvageable material.

'The two in this one were lucky to get out of it alive – getting out unhurt was a bloody miracle,' said Jack.

'You can say that again, Jack,' said the Sergeant. 'You two go and try to remove the undamaged section of the tail-plane – you know how difficult those mitred joints are to get exactly right. And Jack – check the starboard wing to see if there is anything useful on it.'

It proved to be a particularly fruitful salvage operation. The reception committee of insurgents that had welcomed them on their arrival meant they were delayed in starting and the consequence of this was that they had to spend two nights under canvas at the site.

CHAPTER TWELVE

On the evening of the day after Shanin had reported that the caravan was no longer being followed, the life of Kariz was to change beyond anything he could ever have dreamt of, even in his wildest imagination.

He was summoned to the Queen's tent. As he entered he was invited to sit down facing the Queen. This was the first occasion in all the years that he had served the Queen that he had been invited to sit in her presence, and he didn't feel comfortable doing so. He was soon to feel a lot more uncomfortable.

'Kariz, you have known and served me for eleven summers since I was sixteen. What do you think of me?'

'I would give my life to protect you, your majesty.'

'I know that, Kariz, but what do you think of me as a woman? What do you think of my body?'

Kariz felt his cheeks colouring. He hadn't been this embarrassed since his mother caught him doing what he was doing when he was thirteen while he was secretly watching some young women who were bathing in a wadi near Marib. Of course he knew that the Queen was a beautiful woman with body most men would die to possess, and he had on occasions had lustful thoughts about her himself...

Where the courage came from for him to say what he did he didn't know, but in a surprisingly calm voice, he replied:

'It is said by many that you are the most beautiful creature in

all creation, and many would give their lives to possess you. I am no different to that many.'

'*Yes you are, Kariz,*' said the Queen, '*because I am asking you to become the one to possess me. I have been in love with you since my sixteenth summer. After listening to the wisdom of King Solomon I realise that I want you to become my Consort.*'

She touched the back of his hand and he felt a tingling sensation all over his body.

'*Perhaps you would like to return to your tent to contemplate what I have said? Tomorrow I will have my senior advisor declare you as my Consort and then you can take up residence in my tent and in the royal bed.*'

Kariz, in a state of complete but deliriously happy bewilderment, rose, made his customary parting salutations, left the Queen's tent and returned to his own. The following morning all the members of the caravan train were assembled, a temporary dais had been constructed for the Queen, and she was seated on a temporary throne – another empty throne stood beside it. The senior advisor stepped up. There was a buzz of expectation in the assembled crowd. Without any preamble the advisor raised his hand and with a voice of authority which was befitting of his status he announced:

'*Loyal subjects of our majesty, it is my pleasure to announce that the Queen of Sheba has invited commander Kariz – and he has gratefully accepted – to forthwith become her Royal Consort.*'

The stunned silence was followed by a huge roar of approval. Kariz was a very popular person with everyone in the caravan. Zeki, who was standing near him, gave him a congratulatory slap on the back and a few of the soldiers standing nearby, although pleased for him, muttered '*Lucky son of a camel.*' Kariz's men, as he would have expected, stood resolutely to attention at their posts, but even they could not suppress their smiles. The Queen smiled at Kariz and beckoned him to join her and to sit in the throne alongside hers. He mounted the dais and sat down with his Queen. This was greeted with a thunderous roar. This time even the bodyguard detail joined in the congratulations. The Queen placed her hand on the back of Kariz's and once again he experienced the tingling sensation all over his body.

That evening, after a shortened day's trek, there was a party *to celebrate the 'betrothal'. That night Kariz went to the Queen's tent which was now 'their' tent, where the exhilarating tingling sensation that he had experienced when she had touched his hand became an explosion of rapturous pleasure in the royal bed, for both of them. The journey to Marib lasted for another two moons.*

As the caravan approached the town the population ran out to welcome home their Queen. Word of the appointment of a Consort for the Queen spread like a wildfire and people waved and cheered as the cavalcade passed. As soon as the Queen's carriage reached the palace, Solomon's envoy, flanked by four soldiers, stepped forward. Instantly they were surrounded by the bodyguards. This was a move which they had practised many times in the past and Kariz was quite pleased with how effectively they had carried it out. The envoy explained who he was and what he had been instructed to do.

Orders were given. The camels that were carrying the treasure that King Solomon had given to the Queen were brought to the front, had their cargoes unloaded and the treasures were taken into the palace, where they were placed in the main chamber. All attendants, bodyguards and soldiers were instructed to wait outside. The Queen, Kariz and the envoy then inspected the contents of the treasure boxes.

'Where is the object which is wrapped in parchment?' asked the envoy in a voice that betrayed how tense he was.

Kariz pointed to a rolled-up carpet. The envoy eagerly unrolled it to reveal the parchment-wrapped item inside. At first glance the seals appeared to be intact, but of course that couldn't be the case, so he took a much closer look. Solomon had said that they would be broken, and he – being so wise – was always correct, but they did not seem to be damaged in any way. His hands were trembling now. After he had scrutinised the seals for the sixth time he knew that they really had not been broken. How was he going to be able to give this news to the King? He had been absolutely certain that the seals would not be intact.

The envoy informed the Queen and Kariz that his business was now complete and that he would be leaving for Jerusalem the following morning.

Solomon realised that he now had a problem. The trade agreements that he had established with Sheba were very important for his own future prosperity. Taking Sheba by force could prove too costly and – more importantly as far as he was concerned – he had lost the chance to secure the Queen of Sheba for his royal bedchamber. The existence of a consort presented an apparently insurmountable difficulty, yet three days later a solution was to present itself. It was during a session when the King was presiding over representations that had been made to him for his ruling. One of his subjects was brought before him by the families of three different men.

'I want just one spokesman for all of the families to tell me why this woman has been brought before me, and what the charges are that are laid against her.'

Although the King had paused during his pronouncement, the one who had been chosen to speak for them all was careful not to say anything until he was sure that the King had completed what he wanted to say.

'Well?'

'Your majesty, this woman has poisoned three husbands and we are asking' – he had carefully avoided the word 'demanding' – 'that she should answer for her actions.'

King Solomon sat with his elbows on the arms of the throne and his hands clasped so that his nose rested on his forefingers. He sat for quite a while, so long that in fact some of those in the court thought he had fallen asleep. After what seemed an eternity he looked up and said:

'I will hear what this woman has to say in private.'

The court was cleared and the woman stood before him, bound, with her feet shackled.

'Your life depends upon you telling me the absolute truth,' said Solomon. 'If you lie to me you will be subjected to the torturer's whims and then the executioner's blade. Do you understand?'

The woman, who was now trembling uncontrollably, nodded agreement.

'Speak up,' demanded the King.

'Y... y... yes, your Majesty.'

Then it was time for the question that the accused was dreading.

'Did you poison three husbands?'

There was a long pause and her trembling increased. There was no way of avoiding the answer, and so with bowed head, she said in an almost inaudible voice:

'Yes, your Majesty.'

Another long pause while she awaited the inevitable death sentence. It didn't come.

'How was it that the poison was not detected?'

She didn't answer.

'If you want to save your life you had better answer.'

'Save my life?' she thought. 'It was a potion that can't be detected. It was handed down through my family.'

Now it was surprise time.

'Not only will I spare your life, but if you complete the task that I am about to set before you, I will reward you so that you will never have to work again.'

The woman could not believe what she was hearing.

'Of course your Majesty,' she muttered. 'Anything, your Majesty and thank you, your Majesty.'

'You no doubt know of the Queen of Sheba.'

She nodded.

'And her consort Kariz?'

She nodded again.

'Here is what I want you to do. You are to travel to Sheba with my envoy …' He outlined exactly what her task would be, then added: 'If you fail you will be returned here to face the torturer and the executioner's blade.'

The three families that had brought the case to Solomon were very unhappy about his decision not to have the woman executed. They would have been more outraged if they had known what the King had offered her. But after receiving a handsome reward they were quite content to leave the matter there.

The released prisoner joined the caravan of the envoy to Sheba two days later when it set off on its journey south. The envoy had been told that if he made sure that the mission was successful then it would go some way to redeeming his past failure. The problem was that the envoy was not sure what his 'failure' had been.

CHAPTER THIRTEEN

On the morning of the second day, Jack made an early start because he wanted to take a photo of the sun as it came up from behind the small fringe of mountains that he'd observed off to the east. So after the customary check for scorpions in his socks and boots, and before breakfast, Jack dressed and made his way to the eastern perimeter, poised ready to snap the sunrise. He caught it at the instant the sun appeared over the distant mountains. He was quite pleased that he'd been able to catch that moment, and looked forward to seeing how it would turn out. It also made him wish he had one of the new cameras that used rolls of film and took colour photos, but they were well beyond his pocket.

A Corporal in the photography section on the airbase obligingly included Jack's snaps with the official batches of photographs. As he walked back from where he had taken his picture, he was still wondering about the unearthly silence that had occurred at the very moment he had operated the shutter of the camera. The camp was just beginning to come to life as he got back, in time for breakfast.

That morning quite a lot of the fuselage was dismantled and loaded onto one of the trucks. The next procedure was to fix up an anchor post and – using a block and tackle – pull the engine away from the remainder of the crash. The engine was then stripped of any useful parts, which in this case was not very much. The remains of the fuselage were piled in a heap and, in the time-honoured fashion, set on fire. This was a procedure which Jack had experienced on numerous occasions during his spell at the Egypt Depot.

Once the trucks were loaded, it was time for the team to start on its journey back to Khor Maksar. Just before they set off, Jack nipped over to the ruin and picked up three orangey brown coloured stones, each about the size of a cricket ball. There were at least four or five dozen of them scattered around outside the now abandoned khazi. He trotted back to the truck and clambered in. After they had been travelling for about half an hour Sergeant Taylor, who was seated in the cab alongside the driver, looked over his shoulder at Jack.

'What's with the stick and stones?'

'Well someone had taken the trouble to put the stick in a box and bury it in that ruin back there – it's got some Arabic writing on it and I was going to ask Ranjit what it says.'

Jack then passed one of the stones to the Sergeant.

'Don't get it, Jack. It's just an orangey brown stone. There were loads of 'em just scattered about, outside the bog building.

'Give it a shake.'

'Oh yeah – it rattles!'

Then Jack explained how he had discovered that only some of them rattled.

'There were several others that rattled,' he said, 'but I thought that I would take these three back to show Flight Lieutenant Williams. You know how he's interested in this sort of thing.'

It was a long trek back to Aden, about a seventy-mile journey over some rather inhospitable terrain. A stop for the day was made after forty miles, more for the sake of the trucks than the horses of the Aden troop; also it was getting late in the day. The two halves of the deployment camped the usual ten yards apart. That evening, after they had eaten, Jack walked over to the Aden Troop section to ask Ranjit about the writing on the stick.

Jack had seen Ranjit around the base back at Aden and knew him quite well by sight, but there had never been conversation as such between them. Despite the fact that most of the Indian soldiers that made up the Aden Troop spoke some English, there was always segregation between the RAF personnel and the Troop. Apart from the cultural differences, socialisation was frowned up, though never stated. In fact there was talk that somewhere in standing orders it stated that it was against King's Regulations.

As a result of his experiences in Egypt, Jack had developed an inherent distrust of the most of the Arabs – or Ay-rabs as they were usually referred to. The members of the Aden Troop, who originated in India, were considered a lot more trustworthy. His experiences of the past couple of days had made him realise that they were damned good soldiers. And he was aware that Ranjit had been prepared to put his life on the line when he thought that Jack might have been in danger.

The conversation didn't get off to a good start. Ranjit was by nature a very taciturn and a somewhat withdrawn person. So at the beginning it was rather a strained 'chat', but eventually Ranjit came out of his shell and they began to talk about their families and swap tales about past experiences. After a while Jack showed Ranjit the stick and asked him if he could decipher the Arabic carvings on it, and the Arabic writing on the paper. Ranjit said that his Arabic was not all that good, so he called over the Arab guide. The guide took a long look at the stick, while one of Ranjit's men acted as interpreter.

'The carving says that this is the rod of some ancient leader or prophet,' said the guide via his interpreter. 'The writing on the paper is rather unclear – it is something about 'a gift suitable for a queen.'

Jack thanked the guide and handed him a small baksheesh, with which he was highly delighted and thanked Jack effusively. Not long after this Jack returned to his side of the encampment feeling none the wiser and threw the stick into the back of the truck. After breakfast the next day, the salvaging contingent set off on the last lap back to base, crossing the Wadi Bana. They arrived back at Khor Maksar with their booty just as the sun was setting.

A few mornings after getting back to base, Jack collected his developed film and prints from the photography section. The corporal complimented him on the shots that he had taken. 'The ones you took of the salvage operation I'll submit to the Photographic Officer if you don't mind,' he said. 'I'm sure they'll be useful for a procedure manual he's putting together. But you made a bit of a mess with the one of the camel train – it's very blurry and out of focus.'

'Camel train? We didn't see any bloody camel train out in that Godforsaken desert.'

'It's the one that you took after the shot of the burning of non-useful salvage.'

'That should be a sunrise.' Jack looked at the offending picture. 'Bugger! It was a really good sunrise and somehow I've taken a photograph of something that bloody well wasn't there.'

It was several weeks before Jack was able to ask Flight Lieutenant Williams about the orangey brown stones. The Flight Lieutenant expressed a very keen interest in Jack's find.

'I believe that they are probably the result of some prehistoric volcanic eruption at Crater that threw molten lava high into the air, and in some parts it fell like giant incandescent raindrops,' he said. 'Perhaps there was a rainstorm that caused irregular cooling – that could have caused the central parts of the stones to become separated from the outer shell. Why don't we slice one of them open to have a look?'

'A good idea,' said Jack, and it was arranged that he would take one to the workshop after duty the next day. But, it was not to be. The following day – a Friday – Flight Lieutenant Williams, with aircraftsman Davies, went on a bombing sortie. Their plane DH 8031 crashed and they were both killed.

After their funeral service at Maala cemetery, Jack lost interest in the stick and stones. He threw them into his kitbag and forgot all about them, though he did continue with his photography. After a few months he ran out of ideas of what to photograph on the base, so he decided to restrict himself to just taking photos on recovery missions. Quite a few of his shots ended up in the procedure manual that was being compiled by one of the officers.

Despite an extended period of increased bombing and recovery missions, there was still time for play as well as work on the camp. Jack was anything but a 'dull boy'. At one time he joined a group who, motivated by one of the officers who had been a keen yachtsman back home, set about building a land yacht out of scrap material that they managed to acquire, often the leftovers from stuff salvaged from crash sites. The land yacht consisted of an old vehicle chassis with large wheels, a thin mast and a couple of improvised sails. From a distance, with its instantly recognisable lateen sail, the contraption looked like a small beached Dhow. Despite the strong breeze that often blew from the east, it was obvious that the contrivance was never going to break any records, even on the open stretch of reasonably firm stand. In fact it was considered a successful afternoon if it managed to move more than a hundred yards.

Trips into Aden tended to be infrequent. Jack however, on the few occasions when he went into town, always took photographs of the local sights to show the folks back at home – not that there seemed to be much hope of going home for some while yet. One of the sights in Aden that really impressed him were the Water Tanks on the outskirts, where the water supplies for the town were collected and stored. The guide at this particular site of antiquity informed him that the tanks were hundreds of years old and had been built during the rule of the 'Little Queen of Sheba'.

During his time at Khor Maksar, particularly during forages into the hinterland, Jack became increasingly aware of the importance of water. He remembered the ever-welcome wadis, except when they were dry, and the few-and-far-between wells where it cost a farthing for two gallons of fresh water.

The RAF continued to be involved in what appeared to be the never-ending but always changing tribal wars throughout the area, though it did seem that the tribes which the RAF was supporting were gaining the upper hand. Over the next two years, Jack was able to photograph many different desert and mountainous landscapes, as he was involved in numerous different missions all over the southern part of Arabia.

Two years after arriving in Aden, almost to the day, Jack was promoted to leading aircraftman, and a year later he and two others from the base were posted to – of all places – Somaliland; the place where Wing Commander Bowhill had conducted his acts of derring-do which had so excited young

David. Jack recalled that it was Dave's initial recounting of these stories that had been the catalyst which had projected him into his life in the RAF, a life that he now accepted had been, and still was, adventurous and exciting.

He was sad to say goodbye to Gus and Ginger – they had been through some good and bad times over the past eight years. British Somaliland was very different to Aden. Here, there was no longer a war going on, no bombing or rescue and recovery missions. It appeared to Jack that the RAF was there just to be seen. Life was much more leisurely but the location was even more remote. The nearest town, if you could call it that, was Berbera, little more than a coastal fishing village. Expeditions into the surrounding areas were undertaken for leisure rather than for active service. Life had to be lived at a leisurely pace because the temperature was even hotter than in Aden. Although it was only 150 miles south of Aden, where the summers shimmered in the blazing sun at 97° F, Berbera baked in the solar oven at 104° F. Fortunately just ninety miles inland at Burau (Burao) it was warm and dry all year round, and the day time temperature never went above 88° F and never fell below 80° F.

After a couple of weeks, Jack began to wonder what he had done to be given such a cushy posting, but he wasn't going to complain. Although some members of the Aden Troop were already deployed at Berbera, they had very little to do other than 'general duties' because there were no hostilities taking place. During the whole of Jack's tour of duty in Somalia, there was not a single call-out for a recovery operation.

The number of personnel on the base was less than a quarter of that at Khor Maksar, and Jack was pleasantly surprised to discover that airmen (other ranks) were housed in bungalows with four airmen to each. Despite the fact that the bungalows had tin roofs, they were quite luxurious compared with the accommodation Jack had experienced during his time in the RAF. Once again he had one of those sudden realisations, a moment of awareness that we all experience. He had now been an airman for over eight years and he had been away from home for more than four: he had spent half of his time in the RAF overseas.

The bungalows made all of the occupants feel less like servicemen and a bit like African settlers, particularly when they sat outside their bungalows in the evening, like plantation owners but not quite like the 'Happy Valley Set'.

Because the daily workload was very much reduced, it meant that there was plenty of time to venture into the surrounding countryside, which Jack and his fellow airmen did whenever they could, usually in pairs, occasionally in groups of four or more, and sometimes but not always accompanied by an officer. The relatively cooler climate away from the coast, together with the undulating hills and valleys, made it slightly reminiscent of the Downs in the south of England. It was such a change from the rugged escarpments and jagged sawtoothed peaks of the mountains that edged the dusty desert of the Arabian Peninsula, where the terrain looked flat but was deceptively undulating. The liberal scattering of trees that looked like upturned giant witches' brooms on the smoother landscape of Somalia did not detract from the impression of being something more akin to the landscape back home.

Two of the officers on the base who came from well-to-do families organised an unexpected leisure activity: hunting parties. The class divisions back home would have precluded any shared activity like this, but as the saying goes 'necessity makes strange bedfellows,' and this was not 'back home'. Jack was surprised that the officers didn't try to stand on ceremony or cling to their status. Or, as he succinctly put it, 'they're OK – not toffee-nosed buggers trying to lord it over us poor sods.'

The 'hunting parties' were transported in two trucks to Upper Sheik, in the Burau area. The prey was antelope, which were to be found in abundance. Before setting out, the airmen were given authority to collect their rifles and draw live ammunition from the armoury. For Jack and his fellow airmen, this was the only time that they had fired their Lee Enfield 303s, other than on a few rare occasions at the rifle range on the base. These rifles, unlike those with which they had been issued when they were recruits, had firing pins and were kept under lock and key at the armoury.

When the hunting parties arrived at the 'halfway house', as the dropping-off point was known, it was on foot from thereon.

They all were surprised how successful they were at hunting. It was only with hindsight that those who took part in these forays realised why it was so easy to bag a prey. The antelope were not accustomed to being killed at a distance by a gun. The officers who ran this show had an arrangement with one of the locals. In exchange for the carcases he would organise the mounting of the antlers on plaques. During his time at Berbera, Jack had a couple of horns of antelope mounted which he was going to take home with him to show the folks back home. Trophies of the time when he was a 'Great White Hunter'. That was the plan, but of course things don't always go to plan.

Although Jack and his colleagues were enjoying a really easy life, the other side of the coin was that it made the time go very slowly and – truth be known – Jack was quite pleased when six months later he was posted to 208 Squadron based at Abu Seuir in Egypt, about ten miles west of Ismailia, at the bottom end of the Suez canal.

Life proved to be far busier at Abu Seuir. Although it was back to the desert landscape, there was no jagged fringe of menacing mountains. To the east, in the distance, ships could be seen making their way in convoys through the Suez Canal. No longer was there the luxury of being accommodated in bungalows, but the quarters were much better than those in Aden. The temperature was much more tolerable than it had been in Aden and Berbera, too. Jack recalled how he and his fellow airmen had felt when they first arrived in Africa, and how hot they thought it was, but now the climate seemed to be absolutely balmy. What was more to the point, at night it became cool, in fact sometimes cold, which made it much easier to sleep. The khaki shorts and shirts and pith helmets (topee, airman for the use of) were returned to stores and replaced with the old high-neck blue grey uniform.

Because Abu Sueir was the only overseas flying training unit in existence at the time, many training flights were taking place, and as a consequence, there were quite a few crashes. Jack found himself once again involved with recovery operations. Fortunately the terrain was not as inhospitable as it had been in Arabia and the distances from the base to the crash sites were nowhere near as great as those to which he had become

123

accustomed. With so much activity, the time passed much more quickly. The months ticked down like a hyperactive metronome. Christmas quickly came and went.

It was quite common for riggers who had been working on an aircraft to go up on test flights. Often this would be with trainees who had recently been passed as fit to go solo. During the second week in February, Jack was allocated to go on one of these test flights with a recently qualified young pilot. The test flight started out well enough, but after about ten minutes Jack, from his position in the rear cockpit seat, noticed that one of the tension wires appeared to be too slack between two struts on the starboard wing.

'Better take her slowly and gradually as you can back to the runway, sir – one of the struts doesn't look right,' he shouted to the young pilot.

'No, she feels alright, airman. I'll just take her a bit higher and bank her towards the 'drome.'

'Better not, sir.'

'I'm the pilot here,' retorted the still wet-behind-the-ears pilot, getting quite shirty as he started too violent a bank.

'You stupid bugger ... sir,' yelled Jack, and at that moment there was a deafening crack as the strut broke. A highly skilled, experienced pilot might have nursed the aircraft back to the runway. This pilot wasn't and he didn't. He panicked. The next thing Jack saw was the ground, which now seemed to be in the wrong place, and was rushing towards him at an alarming rate. *'This is it,'* he thought.

CHAPTER FOURTEEN

The Queen of Sheba gave birth to a daughter seven moons after she arrived back from Jerusalem, but the joy of the Queen, Kariz and the population was short-lived. Three days after the birth, Kariz died of a mysterious illness. The Queen was totally distraught and absolutely certain that Solomon had something to do with the death of her beloved Consort.

After a long consultation with her senior advisor, who was equally certain as to who was to blame, it was decided that it might be prudent for the Queen to make a journey to the land across the sea. She would go to Ophir from where most of her gold and many of her precious stones came, and stay there for a while, just in case Solomon started to send envoys to Sheba to make more approaches to her. It was agreed that the journey would be far too arduous for her new-born infant. So the latest member of the royal household of Sheba was to be left with a wet nurse and a retinue of carers and bodyguards. Although the Queen hated the thought of leaving her daughter Kalila – her lasting memory of Kariz – behind in Sheba, she knew in her heart of hearts that it was the safest course to action to follow. 'Kalila will probably be walking and talking before I see her again' *was the thought that troubled her the most. The reality was to be worse: she would never see Kalila again.*

Plans for the trip were made, and before the next new moon, early one morning a caravan set out from Marib bound for Ophir. The disappearance of the Queen of Sheba was shrouded in mystery.

The day after the caravan had left Marib there was no sign that it had ever existed.

The failure in his attempts to possess the Queen of Sheba marked a turning point in the life of King Solomon. Despite the fact that he was no longer a young man, he started to take many women, most of them with connections to other royal families, to his bed with what seemed to be an insatiable appetite.

A couple of summers later one of King Solomon's bodyguards, as he lay abed with and was talking to an obliging lady with whom he was spending the night, mentioned what the King was getting up to.

'Ever since he learned of the Queen of Sheba's disappearance, he appears to have lost all of his wisdom. It is said that he has had a different 'so called wife' every night for the past two years.'

'But that's over seven hundred wives,' replied the temporary inamorata more in disbelief than awe – she was well aware of men's capabilities.

'Don't forget the King is well past his prime.'

Nonetheless this was going to be quite a tasty tit-bit of gossip for the market place, and would eventually end up becoming part of the accepted history of King Solomon.

Whether it was a result of all that exertion or his failure to possess the Queen of Sheba, less than eight summers later the King died.

In the meantime, whether someone in the royal household of Sheba had started to use the rod or not is debatable, but over the following few decades many new springs mysteriously appeared, pouring water into the river that flowed through Marib. Irrigation systems were constructed and a dam was built, and the verdant area became progressively larger and more verdant. As a result Marib became more and more prosperous. It was as if the Queen of Sheba had handed over to her descendants the responsibility of making sure that there was always a plentiful supply of water.

❦

The sands of time were blown across the desert in an incessant but ever-changing manner, constant but irregular, ever-seeking infinity. Forty lifetimes passed, marking the passage of a millennium. The

Great Marib dam collapsed, flooding the land of Sheba, which began its journey back to being a desert town. Another forty lifetimes completed their journeys, marking the passing of another millennium, at which time another great ruler took over the role that once had been the Queen of Sheba's. This was at a time when the 'Normans' were conquering a distant small island.

In a similar manner to that of her distant predecessor, Queen Arwa al-Sulayhi – the little Queen of Sheba, as she was known – arranged the building of many fountains in Marib. She also had 'water tanks' built in Aden, the port in the south of Sheba.

Had the rod that produced water been handed down through all of those generations? Had she used it? Water did seem to be again over plentiful in the area.

❦

Queen Arwa al-Sulayhi, the little Queen of Sheba, had ruled the land for nearly forty summers and had managed through astute leadership to keep the loyalty of the local chieftains. Sheba consisted of nine ill-defined tribal states. As a symbol of her authority over the land she had had a golden crown made with nine equal-sized rubies, each of them the size of a chicken's egg, one ruby per tribe, and as such the crown was worth a great deal more than its considerable monetary value.

There had been signs of increased tension and unrest in the land of Sheba for more than ten moons, and it had reached a point where the whole region seemed to be on the verge of descending into a state of turmoil, chaos and conflict. What had triggered this unrest was the death of the Queen's only daughter: she had died in childbirth together with the baby. This was made more significant by the fact that, fifteen summers before, both of Arwa al-Sulayhi sons had been killed by robbers during a visit to Ophir. There was now no obvious successor to the throne. Two chieftains from the north were vying to become the next overall ruler of the Federacy. Although they each thought that they should be the next sovereign of Sheba, the leaders of the other tribes distrusted both of them and were becoming more and more concerned about the future.

It was during one of the regular consultations that the Queen had with her chief advisor, who had been a loyal confidant for more summers than she wished to remember, when she looked at him with a very worried expression and said in an unfaltering voice which belied her age: 'Hakim, we live in perilous times. With all the dissent that is taking place, I am concerned that when the time comes for me to depart this life, because I have no direct descendant or suitable successor to take my place, Sheba is likely to disintegrate and crumble away to nothing.'

The advisor was quiet for some while, before he replied.

'The two rival chieftains of the north will never be reconciled, and neither of them would make a suitable ruler for Sheba,' he said. 'Your majesty, it is with a heavy heart that I have to say that I believe what you have said is absolutely correct, and the days of our beloved Sheba may well be coming to an end. My spies in the north tell me that before two or possibly three moons have passed there will be an attack on Marib and one of the Chieftains will try to seize the crown.'

Arwar al-Sulayhi, in the manner of her advisor, was silent for a while. A 'just as I thought' expression rested on her face.

'Neither the nine-tribe crown, nor the rod of the ancient leader must be allowed to fall into the hands of either of those chieftains,' she said. 'This is what I want to be done ...'

That night under the cover of darkness three members of the Queen's household, three of her most trusted subjects, left the palace carrying two boxes. They made their way to an unoccupied pottery on the southern outskirts of the city. Once there, one of them removed some of the flat stones on the floor, dug a hole and buried the long box. He then replaced the flat stones and scattered the sandy soil which had been excavated, outside the building. In the meantime the other two, who were visibly shedding tears, rekindled the small firing kiln, took the nine-tribe crown out of its box and removed all the large rubies in turn, and wrapped each of them in small pieces of cloth. Then using some pottery clay, they encased the rubies so that they resembled irregular balls about the size of a fist. They also moulded about fifty similar sized balls without any of the revered rubies inside. They gradually built up the fire. One of them had seen it done before when he had helped his brother to make pots in his workshop. It was not until about an hour before dawn that they were able to remove the balls from the kiln and carefully scatter them outside, near the discarded shards of failed pottery, so that they could slowly cool. The sun was just about peering over the edge of the horizon when they arrived back at the palace. The crown, now sans rubies, was taken to an alchemist, melted down and moulded into a bar.

Not out of fear for her own life, but out of fear for what would become of Sheba, Arwa al -Sulayhi decided to leave, so that when either of the two chieftains of the north attacked Marib, they would not be able to capture her and hold the other loyal chieftains to ransom. She decided to go to Ophir, as had her illustrious ancestor according to the legend that had been passed down from generation to generation for two millennia.

Because of the imminent threat of an attack on Marib before the next new moon, she set out for the port in the south, with a few members of her royal household servants and a small retinue of bodyguards. So it was that on what proved to be a fateful day, a small camel train of only ten camels left the city just before dawn. A young goat-herd was the only witness to a very strange happening shortly after the Royal camel train had started out; in fact it had travelled less than five thousand paces.

'The sun had just risen and I saw the Queen's caravan heading towards the south,' he said. 'It was about five hundred paces from where the goats were just starting to graze. Then I noticed a black dot in the sky near where the sun had just risen. It looked too big to be a hawk, and as it descended quickly, with a motion like a snake, it grew larger and larger until it looked like the mouth of a cave, and it stopped right in front of the caravan, and near two of the goats. I fell to the ground and covered my head with my arms, but my curiosity got the better of me so I took a quick look. The whole caravan and cave entrance and two goats had disappeared. There were just a few swirls of sand spinning up into the sky where the caravan had been.'

When the young goat-herd gave this account to some of the remaining elders in Marib none of them believed him.

'He's just concocted this fantasy as an excuse for letting a wolf or leopard take the two goats,' they said.

He was given ten lashes for losing the goats and a further ten for telling lies to the elders.

The fears of Arwa al-Sulayhi were well founded. The reality for Sheba was in fact worse than the fate that she had envisaged.

The most belligerent of the northern chieftains invaded as soon as he heard of the Queen's disappearance. His tribesmen conducted a campaign of rape, pillage and brutality in their extensive search for the 'nine tribes' crown. Their efforts were doomed from the very beginning, primarily because the three highly trusted subjects who had stayed behind in Marib were callously killed on the first day of the attack on the city. Perhaps if they had been tortured, as was the custom, they may well have divulged what had happened to the coveted crown.

Something else very strange occurred within a few days of the disappearance of the Queen: the springs and wells in Marib began to dry up. In frustration, the northern chieftain laid waste to the city and consigned Sheba to the substance of legend and historical speculation.

CHAPTER FIFTEEN

He opened his eyes but the light was very bright, so he closed them to a squint, to try to stop the pain in his head. When he moved it hurt just about everywhere, so he decided not to move. Why wasn't his brain working? Then gradually he began to remember, if you could call it that, some of what had happened. This couldn't be heaven, he reasoned: *'after what I've done in my past there's no way that I could have got past St Peter, unless I found a back door.'* He liked that idea. *'Yes this was heaven, and I've got in by the back door. But if this is heaven why am I hurting so much?'*

'He showed some signs of coming round a little while ago,' said a female voice.

'I think he's almost conscious now, Sister,' came the answer from a male voice. 'Can you hear me, Toulson?'

Jack heard a croaky voice reply:

'Of course I can. Do you have to bloody well shout? I've got a bleeding thundering headache.'

Jack then realised that it was his voice. He was sorry that it was not heaven and the all-over pain added to his regret.

'You should consider yourself very lucky, Toulson,' continued the voice in an agitated tone.

'Lucky!' thought Jack. *'If you were hurting like I am you wouldn't bloody well think of yourself as lucky.'*

It turned out that Jack had a broken leg, broken arm,

broken collar bone, slight fracture of the skull and several fractured ribs, numerous bruises and abrasions – he was a mess. Later, when he discovered what had happened, he felt sorry for having sworn at the young pilot, because he hadn't survived the crash.

Jack was not allowed out of hospital until the last day of March. But then he was given the good news: he was being posted home to England. Within a week he was aboard a British India ship bound for Blighty. He, together with about two dozen others from the Egyptian Depot, boarded the ship at Port Said. On board there were already over fifty RAF and Army personnel who had embarked either in Bombay or Aden. Jack still had a leg in plaster, and although he no longer required a sling for his arm, he still needed a crutch to get about. One of his mates on the base had packed his kit bag for him. Unfortunately there had not been room for the antelope antlers. Jack thought about leaving the old stick and the three rattling stones behind, but in the end decided to take them home with him. As he still had a leg in plaster, he was put in a cabin alongside the ship's doctor's, on the upper deck. Jack's berth doubled as the doctor's surgery during the day. Nevertheless it was considerably better than the cabins below deck, each of which had to be shared by two servicemen. Next to the cabin in which Jack was to travel home was an RAF Flying Officer. If it had been on an airbase, Jack and the officer would barely have noticed each other except at saluting distances, but under the unusual circumstances, Jack socialised with the officer, who was returning from a two-year deployment in Cairo.

Before the ship had reached Gibraltar the ship's doctor removed the plaster cast from his leg – much to Jack's relief, because under the plaster his leg had itched like mad. Most of his bruises had disappeared and his breathing was becoming much easier and less painful. All was going well with the world. In Gibraltar his mail from home caught up with him after being forwarded twice. He learnt in a letter from his sister Cissy that his mother had died on the day that he had been in the air crash.

Jack arrived back in England at the King George V docks almost five years to the day after he had left from Manston for foreign parts: how things had changed in those five years!

He was granted two weeks of compassionate leave combined with convalescence leave, but of course he was too late for his mother's funeral. Cissy had taken charge of the running of the house. They all appeared to be much more than five years older, particularly the Old Man who looked to be a shell of the man that Jack remembered. They were all pleased to see Jack.

'Aye oop lad, I see tha's walkin' wi' limp, what's tha been oop to?' asked his father.

Jack gave them an edited version of the crash, making it out to be a minor event and avoiding mention of the fact that the pilot had been killed.

Not much had changed in the poverty-furnished room, but more importantly – despite the absence of his mother – there was still the sense and feeling of being a family.

The next day, which was a Sunday, he went with the Old Man, his brother and sisters to the cemetery to pay his respects to Mother. Jack noticed the tears in the eyes of his dad when he said 'I dug Mother's grave, son, t' make sure 'twas done proper.' The word son was not missed by Jack. Knowing what a proud man his father was, Jack was very careful about what he said next.

'Can I 'elp thee wi cost of Mother's 'eadstone?' he said, relapsing into the dialect which had gradually deserted him during his time in the RAF.

'Aye tha can that lad, t' would be reet champion.'

Jack had sent money home regularly over the past five years, but had saved enough to help the family even more now that he was back home.

Jack was the eldest, then there was Cissy – she was now twenty-five – then Doris, who was two years younger than her sister. Jack's brother Alan had just had his twentieth birthday, and the youngest – Annie – would be eighteen in a few weeks' time. Both Doris and Annie worked in the button factory and Alan had a job in the steelworks. Cissy had left the button factory to look after the home. It emerged during the conversations that Cissy was courting a shopkeeper's son over in Attercliffe, and Jack realised that it would not be too long before she would want to leave and set-up a home with her young man. All of the girls of her age, those that she had gone to school with, were already married except Agnes Sidebottom who was quite plain or – to be downright honest- had a face that could launch a thousand nightmares, and a personality to match, plus a personal hygiene problem.

Jack had brought home a few souvenirs – colourful rugs from Aden, carved animals from Cairo, a bottle of eau de cologne for each of his sisters, a model of a Ninack made out of brass, which he had spent many hours making during his time in Aden, for his brother, and a proper pipe for his dad to replace the clay pipes that he was forever breaking, together with some baccy. He had taken the precaution of not buying the tobacco until he arrived back in England. He knew his Old Man wouldn't like that 'foreign muck'. That evening, as the two of them sat smoking in the scullery, the Old Man with his new pipe and Jack with his Woodbines, Jack mentioned to his dad that he hadn't bought the tobacco abroad.

'I knew you wouldn't like the stuff that they smoke in Egypt – it smelt like burning camel dung, and the stuff that the French smoked didn't even didn't smell that good.'

It was good to see his Old Man smile through the grief and pain-carved lines on his face.

'I see tha's gone over to wearing 'obnail boots now, Dad.'

'Aye, took a while t' get used t' them but now they're reet comfy.'

Jack left the shawl that he had bought for his mother in his kit bag with the rattling stones and the old stick. The sisters had fixed the rugs on the wall of the scullery, which brightened up the room considerably. Initially Jack had been disappointed that his hunting trophies had been left behind at Abu Seuir, but he realised how out of place they would have looked in the Sheffield 'back to back' tenement. Possibly they might have looked at home in poor young Dave's parents' house, '*but not here*' thought Jack. And then as an afterthought, '*I wonder what has happened to his mother and father?*'

One evening after they had finished their meal – Jack

noted that Cissy had turned out to be a good cook, just like her mother – as they were all crowded in the small scullery, Jack showed them the old stick with the Arabic message carved on it and one of the rattling stones. He always showed them off the same way and it was always the same reaction.

'But it's just an old orangey stone.'

'Try shaking it.'

'Oh yes, it rattles.'

Jack told them to keep the stone to show their friends and neighbours because he had two others. The stick didn't seem to interest them, even with all the gibberish carved on it, nor the odd writing on the piece of paper that was with it, so Jack stuffed them back into his kitbag with mother's shawl.

Towards the end of the leave, with the Old Man's permission, for a treat he took them all to see the first of the new talkies, *The Jazz Singer* starring Al Jolson, at the Regent cinema, in the middle of the city opposite the City Hall. To get there they went 'on t' tram'. They all really enjoyed the new experience, especially when the Wurlitzer organ was played before the film was shown. However when Al Jolson sang 'Mammy' the three girls cried their eyes out; Jack, his dad and brother brushed their eyes repeatedly with the backs of their forefingers, as they remembered Mother.

A few days after this treat it was time for Jack to say goodbye. When the time came, he quickly made his farewells and set off for RAF Hendon, back to the base where he had been stationed before being sent to Egypt. The two weeks' leave had come to an end all too soon in one sense, because he hadn't seen his family for so long and there had been a lot of catching up to do: nevertheless he was keen to get back to what he had spent years training to do and which he enjoyed doing. It was ten weeks since the crash and Jack was almost over his injuries, but on his arrival at Hendon, the MO gave him an 'excused parades' chit, and it was a further month before he resumed all normal duties.

At the end of October he was posted to RAF Manston; it was almost as if he was retracing his steps in reverse. This time the experience was much more pleasant, made even more satisfying because he was promoted to Corporal. But, as the saying goes, 'you can't escape your past'. There were some on the base who remembered him and word soon got round. A bit like the return of the prodigal son, here was the return of 'the bloke who shagged Eunice'. Jack realised there was no point in trying to deny it, even though it was not true. And after a few weeks the jokes faded and life resumed a normal pattern.

Four weeks after his arrival back a Manston, Jack was given a 72-hour weekend pass, so he decided to pay a visit to George and Esme. It had been nearly eight years since he had seen them. On the Saturday afternoon, as he was on his way to Blean and changing buses in Ramsgate, he was surprised to see that the rock factory was still open, even though it was late November and quite chilly. Although no rock was being made there was still plenty for sale, so Jack bought a big bag full. This time the journey to Blean was much more comfortable than when he'd gone to try to bring back Dave – the buses were faster and had padded seats. When he arrived at their cottage, he was surprised to discover that Mary and Brian now had two baby sisters. *'Fortunate that I bought all that rock,'* thought Jack.

George and Esme were overjoyed to see him but the two youngest children were a little wary, and for about quarter of an hour they hung very close to their mum and eyed Jack with suspicion. When he produced the large bag of rock their suspicion melted. 'Uncle Jack' suddenly became their best friend, and their allegiance to their mum suddenly became transferred to Jack.

He regaled them with tales of what he had seen in Africa and Arabia. Even George, who had seen time on the Western Front in the Great War, was impressed by Jack's account.

'Did you see the Pyramids? Did you ride on a camel? Did you see Tutankhamun's coffin?' The questions tumbled out in what appeared to be a never-ending flow.

Jack produced some of the photographs he had taken. Mary was particularly interested in these, but her brother Brian was far more interested in hearing about the aircraft. The two younger sisters Alice, who was five years old, and Eileen who was three, were definitely more interested in the rock.

When he had been planning a visit to the family, he

remembered that it would be just after Mary's ninth birthday. He had intended to buy a present for her when he went into Ramsgate to catch the Canterbury bus, but there hadn't been any toyshops open. This placed him in a difficult situation. He realised that the rock he had bought would not really be suitable. Then he had what he hoped was a face-saving idea. He had brought the stick and a stone along with the intention of showing the family some of the items that he had collected on his travels. The change of plan was to give the stick to Mary, and as he could hardly take a gift for Mary and not give anything to Brian he would give him the stone. Of course, he hadn't known about their younger sisters but they seemed well satisfied with the rock.

'This is a sort of a late birthday present for you, Mary,' said Jack, thinking *'I suppose this isn't really a suitable present for a little girl.'* 'I found it buried just like a treasure – in Arabia.' He took the stick with the strange writing on it out of its newspaper wrapping and handed it to her. He also gave her the envelope which contained the piece of paper that he'd found with the stick.

His fear that it was not the right present for a nine-year-old little girl was reinforced and amplified by the silence of Mary when he gave her the stick. Trying to make the gift appear more acceptable to her, he said: 'The Arabic writing on the paper that goes with it says it's a gift fit for a queen.'

Jack need not have been worried about the present – it was not disappointment that had made her silent. She was in a state of excited shock. The blank look changed to a beaming face as a smile swept across it, like the sun coming out from behind a cloud.

'Oh Uncle Jack – it's absolutely wonderful. A real Arabian staff. Miss Johnson, our teacher, says that's what they are called. She reads to us every Tuesday from the Thousand and One Tales of the Arabian Nights, about Sher-hara-sard, about Sinbad the sailor, Aladdin and his wonderful lamp, Ali Baba and the forty thieves, about genies and magic carpets. When I show this, she will be as excited as me.'

The speed with which the words came tumbling out, each one fruitlessly trying to overtake the one in front, was a testament to how excited she was by what Jack had considered to be no more than an interesting old stick.

The response from Brian, when Jack handed him the stone, was nowhere near as effusive – even after he had heard it rattle. Obviously it wasn't much of a gift, so Jack made a mental note that on his next visit he would bring Brian the small brass model which he was making out of scrap in the workshop, a model of the latest Supermarine S5 airplane – the one that had taken part in the Schneider Trophy races.

Later he told them about the time when he had taken a photograph of a camel train that wasn't there. That held them spellbound for a while. There was so much to catch up with that they lost all sense of time and Jack missed the last bus back into Canterbury. George and Esme told Jack that although they didn't have another bed, they would make up the sofa so that he could sleep on it. They also made it quite clear they would not take 'no' for an answer. Sleeping in the barn was not even hinted at, so Jack slept that night on the sofa, which turned out to be quite comfortable. Perhaps it was the surroundings and the meeting up with George and Esme, but what would have been a good night's sleep was disturbed by a vivid dream in which Dave was talking to George about life in the RAF. After a good breakfast Jack bid farewell to them all, promised to come and see them again soon and caught the bus into Canterbury. The journey back to Manston took quite a while, and it was not only because the buses were running to a Sunday timetable. He didn't know it then, but it was going to be almost a year before he would make the journey back to Blean.

CHAPTER SIXTEEN

Pivotal points in life are never predictable. They occur at unexpected times and places, and are decided by fate and time themselves. This bus journey was to be one of those times and places for Jack. Two stops before arriving at the last stop at the 'Pav', a young lady boarded the bus. Jack, who was not a 'ladies man', was instantly attracted to her. She sat in a seat across from him and one row in front. He didn't take his eyes off her for the rest of the journey.

As he alighted from the bus behind her he said 'excuse me, miss – could you tell me where I might be able to get a cup of tea in town on a Sunday?' His plan to return immediately to Manston had now been abandoned.

'Well everywhere is shut on Sunday but I am just on my way to Mass at Saint Augustine's, and after Mass some of the ladies make tea.'

'Would you mind if I accompanied you to the church?' Jack asked.

'No, I suppose that would be alright,' she said.

Back in Sheffield, Jack's family had been Chapel-goers and up until the time he went to sea he had regularly accompanied them. He had never been into a Catholic church, and he was a bit bemused by the service. He was nearly caught out a couple of times by what he later described as the 'bobbing up and down' – kneeling down, standing up, sitting down, and bowing in what seemed to be no prearranged order. When the congregation responded in Latin to the proclamations by the 'reverend' on the altar, Jack indulged in a bit of miming. He was interested to see and of course smell –without coughing – the incense being used, which reminded him of a time when he had looked through the open doors of a Coptic church in Cairo. After the Mass, Jack thought that he had earned the cup of tea. Courting was hard work.

It turned out that the young lady's name was Margaret, and Jack lost no time in asking her if she would like to go to the picture-house in town the next Saturday.

'It'll be my treat for you helping to get me a cup of tea,' he said.

She pretended to be thinking about it for a while, and then said with a shy smile that she would meet him outside the picture-house at six o'clock. Their first date very nearly didn't happen because there was a crash on the base on the Thursday and Jack was in charge of a team to deal with the damaged aircraft. He managed to get the job completed with less than an hour to spare.

Margaret's family was known in Ramsgate because many were members of the Ramsgate lifeboat crew. She was nineteen and had two sisters and three brothers. Two of the brothers worked on fishing boats based in the harbour and lived with their wives in Ramsgate. The other brother, who had given up working on the boats a couple of years previously because of the poor and uncertain wages, had become a miner at the new Betteshanger coal mine near Deal: he was still single and lived at home. Margaret had only vague recollections of her two elder brothers who had been killed in the Great War.

When Christmas leave came round, Jack went to visit his family in Sheffield and during that leave he told them that he was 'walking out' with Margaret. As he told them about her, he realised that – although he had only known her for a few weeks – she was the one for him. So when they met outside the picture-house on the Saturday following his return from leave, he took hold of her hand and said 'Maggie, I've been thinking. Isn't it about time that I met your mum and dad?'

So it was that two weeks later she nervously took Jack

to meet the entire family, apart from the brother who was working a late shift down the mine. Margaret's family – like Jack's -was no stranger to poverty. Her father reminded Jack very much of his own dad. The firm handshake they exchanged didn't go unnoticed by either of them. It soon became apparent that Margaret's dad, like his own, was a strong independent character who was struggling to keep his family off 'the parish'. But her dad's situation was even more difficult, because he could only manage to get occasional work on boats in the harbour. Although he supplemented his earnings by shrimping with a net in the shallow water close to the beach for hours on end, and also did some beachcombing when the tide or season was not right, money was always short. Margaret and her sisters had had jobs as daily domestics in various large houses in town since they had left school. The money that they and their brother brought in just managed to keep the family off the breadline.

When daughters bring young men home to meet the family, most mothers view any young man with suspicion. It was no different in Jack's case. His visit started with a very awkward first quarter of an hour which was filled with many periods of silence. It was not until he mentioned that for four years he had worked on a trawler out of Grimsby that the conversation really took off.

After this first visit to the family, Jack met up with Margaret almost every weekend and they were referred to by all as a 'walking out' couple. It was the Saturday just after Easter, as they were making their way back from the picture-house, when Jack said, completely out of the blue:

'I think we should tell our families that we're going to get married.'

'But you haven't asked me, Jack.'

'Oh sorry, Maggie love – will you marry me?'

Again the pause of the long pretence – then she smiled. 'Of course I will, Jack.'

When they got to Margaret's home, she stood holding Jack's hand, and excitedly told the family about his proposal and her acceptance. After Jack had left to go back to Manston, her mum sat with her in the scullery with a very worried look on her face.

'He's not a Catholic, is he?' she asked, even though she already knew the answer.

'No he's not, Mum,' said Margaret, 'but he's the one I want.'

'But you know that you're not twenty-one yet and you need our approval.'

'But you wouldn't stop me would you, Mum?'

'You're not in the family way are you, Marge?'

'No, Mum! How could you think that?'

'Well it happened to your cousin Daisy. Remember?'

'Yes, Mum, but I'm not like her.'

Margaret could hear the relief in her mum's voice as she said: 'Well, I must admit that Jack seems very nice and we all quite like him. I'm sure I can persuade your dad to agree, but you will have to have a word with Father O'Flaherty about it, because I am not sure that he will marry you and Jack, him not being a Catholic.'

A few weeks later, Margaret – with Jack in tow – went to see the priest at St Augustine's. The meeting didn't get off to a very good start. It was well known that the priest, like most of his colleagues, didn't approve of mixed marriages, and anyone overhearing the exchanges between Jack and the priest would have been bemused by the combination of the priest's Irish brogue and Jack's lapses into his native dialect during moments of frustration. Nevertheless, by the end of the interview – or, more accurately, the interrogation – he was won over by Jack's persuasive manner and agreement that any children that he and Margaret had would be brought up as Catholics.

'Right, my son,' said Father O'Flaherty. 'I think you are a man of integrity, so I will marry you and Margaret. But make sure you don't try to stop her coming to Mass or go back on your word about the education of your children.' Margaret blushed at the mention of children. 'You look like someone who keeps their word,' he said, adding a rather uncharitable afterthought: 'I wish I could say the same about some of my parishioners.'

Jack was just about to say 'thank you, reverend' when he remembered that Margaret had said that he should address the priest as 'Father', so he did – but felt a bit self-conscious doing so.

Margaret told Jack that Father O'Flaherty's decision to perform the marriage was a great relief to her and her mum. The two of them, with the other two sisters, attended Mass regularly at St Augustine's, and they all would have been bitterly disappointed if Margaret had not been able to get married there.

The banns were read and the wedding took place on the last Saturday of July. It was a very quiet affair. There were only fifteen people present including the priest: Margaret, her mum and dad, her two sisters and three brothers, two sisters-in-law, Jack with another Corporal who was his 'best man', and two inquisitive ladies of the parish who had wandered in to see what was happening.

Margaret wore a white high-collar long-sleeved blouse with a powder blue calf-length skirt and a white silk shawl to cover her head. The shawl was a family heirloom handed down from her grandmother, which her mum had worn for her own wedding, and was intended to eventually be worn by all female members of the family on their wedding days.

A few weeks after the wedding, Jack took Margaret to see his friends in Blean. Brian, now eight years old, was far more impressed with the model airplane: the rattling stone had long since been discarded and relegated to a corner of the back garden. Before the year was out, Jack was posted to the RAF College in Cranwell where he and Margaret managed to rent lodgings in nearby Sleaford and a year later they had their first child – a son. The distance and pressures of everyday life meant that the contacts between George, Esme and family and Jack, Margaret and their family gradually became less and less frequent.

Mary was a very bright child and pretty with it, so much so that in 1933, at the age of thirteen, she was made the May Queen of the village. The 'Uncle Jack staff', as she had called it, was still one of her treasured possessions. When she was told that she was to be Queen of the May, she remembered what he had said about the staff being 'a gift fit for a queen', so she took it with her on the carnival float in the procession around the village. She had planned to have her staff in one hand and the rattling stone as an orb in the other, like on the Queen Victoria statue in Canterbury. But Brian, typical of a boy, couldn't remember where he had put the stone. Actually, he had thrown it away in the garden.

It was a very hot year and there was a drought. George's work was becoming more and more difficult because there was hardly any grass for the cows to graze on. The fields had taken on their flaxen hues earlier than anyone could remember. Some of the winter hay feed was already being used and it was only the middle of August. The vegetable garden was in sorry state because the water in the butts, which they used to water the plants, had long since been used up. Every day it took longer and longer to draw water from the pump in the back garden. Mary was a sensitive young soul, and she became very concerned especially after she heard her mum and dad talking about the lack of rain.

'The farmer said that if things don't improve soon, Es, 'e might 'ave to 'ave the 'erd slaughtered,' said her dad. 'I would lose my job and we would lose our 'ome.'

Esme uncharacteristically often became quite abrupt with the children. When they were not helping around the house or garden, they often all played together in the wood at the top of the slope at the far end of 'four acre' field. Mary was to remember this day for the rest of her life. It was 14 August, Eileen's eighth birthday, a Monday, and they were playing in their usual area. The day before, at church, the vicar had been talking about the drought that was on everyone's mind – he then told the story of Mosses at Meribah when he had struck the rock and water had gushed forth.

Mary kept the envelope that contained the paper with the writing on it in a small drawer that was hers in the bedroom which she shared with her sisters. The 'staff' resided in a cupboard in the kitchen.

On this particular day Mary had brought the staff with her and they were playing at re-enacting what Moses had done. With her brother and sisters standing behind her, she struck a moss-covered rock near their favourite oak tree, and said in a loud voice 'let there be water.' Nothing happened. They all sat down with crestfallen long faces and stared at the rock.

'I didn't think it would work,' said Brian

'I thought it might for my birthday,' said Eileen.

Mary stood up 'Well we tried. It would have been nice, but I guess that it was not meant to be.' Then, imitating what she had heard her mother say a number of times, as youngsters are prone to do, she said: 'Oh Lord, we sure could use some water,' at the same time absentmindedly tapping the staff on the rock.

Still feeling rather despondent they decided to go and play by the silver birch trees a bit lower down. They were just about to get up when Alice cried out.

'Look, Mary! Isn't that wet on my shoe?'

They all looked – it was. Within a short space of time the hollow at the base of the tree where they had been sitting became damp and they all started trying to push their feet into the soil.

'It feels all squidgy!' exclaimed Eileen.

It was, in fact, quite soggy and becoming soggier by the second. After less than a minute the hollow began to take on the appearance of a small pond – but not for long. In what seemed no time at all it was a large pond over ten feet in diameter; then the water started to spill over the edge and seep away downhill towards 'four acre' field. Despite this, the pond remained full. Brian had found a broken branch and was trying to scratch a channel in the soil to direct the water, but the water was pouring out so fast that he couldn't keep up with it.

'This water would be useful for the garden,' announced Mary. 'Let's go and tell Mum what has happened, and get some pails to fill the water butts.'

Mary as usual, because she was the eldest, was in charge. Excitedly they ran down through the dried grass of the field, almost as if they were skipping. When they reached the cottage, their mum was in the back garden taking the washing off the line – Monday was always wash-day, and on this day it had taken almost half an hour to pump up enough water.

'Mummy! Mummy! We've found some water,' yelled out Eileen as soon as she caught sight of her mum.

'What's this all about?' asked Esme as her brood quickly surrounded her.

They all tried to talk at once.

Mary's sensible voice cut through the excited babble:

'We've found a pond up in the wood at the other end of four acre field.'

'What do you mean – found a pond? There's no water up in that wood.'

'Yes there is, yes there is!' they all chorused.

'Mary did it with her stick,' added Alice, who was normally the quiet one. 'Just like the vicar said about Moses yesterday.'

'Don't be silly, my dear, that was just a story from the Bible.'

'But it's true, it's true, Mummy' replied Alice tearfully.

'There there, my dear, don't get upset – just let me put this washing in the kitchen and I'll come and see what it's all about.'

They all made their way across the field up to the wood. In their excitement, the children, wanting to get there quickly, were almost dragging their mum along. They were in for almost as much a surprise as their mother was. Before they reached the edge of the field it was already becoming wet underfoot. When they reached the wood they could see that there was now a stream at least three feet wide and a few inches deep flowing with a rolling like motion across the north eastern corner of the field, and beginning to fill the ditch on the eastern boundary. When they reached the oak tree Esme stopped and stared in utter disbelief at the pond from which all of the water was coming.

She didn't say anything for several seconds then she said: 'quickly, you lot – run home and get the pails from the shed behind the privy. We'll fill the water butts with this water.'

'That's what I said,' added Mary, a little piqued because that had been her idea.

With that, all of the children ran to the cottage. Esme remained at the pond, almost as if she was standing guard to make sure it didn't disappear as mysteriously as it had appeared. Play was forgotten for the rest of the day. The children made trip after trip across the field with pails half filled with water and completely filled all the water butts, and watered all the parched plants in the garden.

When George arrived home at teatime, before he had reached the gate all the family ran to greet him. With everyone again talking at the same time it was quite a while before he got the gist of what they were trying to tell him. Although he was hungry after a hard day's work, he wanted to go and see for himself what they were so excited about. Like Esme, he was speechless when he saw the pond and stream, which by now was a little deeper. His first thoughts were about all the water that was going to waste.

'Es – we will have to fill all the water ...'

Before he finished what he was going to say, Esme interrupted.

'The kids have already filled all the water butts.'

The whole family went back down to the cottage with the sun making its way to the horizon, shining on their faces with enough warmth to give them a glow and a euphoric feeling within.

As they chatted while they were eating their evening meal, the whole atmosphere within the cottage was ecstatic. George listened to the animated conversation of how the day's events had unfolded. When Mary talked about striking the rock with the stick he was quiet for a while.

'This is what I reckon 'appened,' he eventually said. 'When you 'it that rock with the stick it moved slightly, and it'd been covering a spring. Moving it allowed the water to come gushing out. Better if we keep miracles for the Bible.'

Mary nodded in agreement but in her heart of hearts she knew that her dad's explanation was not what had really happened, and he could tell from the expression on her face that she didn't think his interpretation of the events was the correct one. He didn't say any more about the appearance of the water because the truth of the matter was that he wasn't really sure himself.

'By the way, where did you put your stick?'

'I ... er ... put it ...' She then remembered that she had dropped it up in the wood near the oak tree when they had first run down to tell her mother about the miraculous appearance of the water. 'I've left it up in the wood,' she said with a very worried look on her face.

'Don't worry, love – I'll have a look for it after we've finished tea. There's still quite a bit of light left so I want to go and have a look to see if I can channel more of that water on to four acre field.'

'Dad, can I come with you?' asked Mary.

It was agreed that Mary and Brian could go with their dad. They spent over an hour up in the wood and in the field. George, with Brian and Mary's help, dug a few shallow ditches and used some old piping to channel some of the water so that it irrigated almost three quarters of four acre field; however, Mary didn't find her staff. It seemed so sad that such a great day should end on an unhappy note.

The next morning, Brian was out of bed bright and early. Although it was the school holidays, the children – even the youngest – got up at the usual time so that they could help their mum by doing jobs in the cottage or in the garden. On this particular morning Brian was up even earlier. He made an appearance downstairs just after his dad had left to go to work, which of course was always very early. As he made his way out of the door his mum called out.

'Where are you off to, sunshine? You haven't had your breakfast yet.'

'I won't be long, Mum I'm just nipping up to the wood to have a quick check on the pond.'

That was true, as far as it went. The real purpose of his going up to the wood was to look for Mary's staff; he knew how much she treasured it.

He spent over half an hour searching all around the area of the pond without success. He then decided to follow the newly created stream, in case it had fallen into the water. All the way across the corner of four acre field the stream no longer had a grassy bottom. The water had scoured out a path down into the soil and it was nearly a foot deep in places. He could see that the system his dad had used to allow the water to seep onto the field was working well. He continued his search along the path of the stream. The ditch was now full of water to a depth of almost two feet. The water had overflowed the ditch just a few yards further along the boundary, and when he got there Brian could see that the water was now pouring into what had been the dried-up bed of the stream and which was now being restored to life.

Hopes of finding his sister's staff were beginning to fade. He decided that he would walk along the path alongside the stream for a little way. He made his way to the gate of the field and then back to where 'Mary's stream', as he had named it, came out of the field. He looked back towards the ditch. Then to his sheer delight and total surprise he saw it, caught in some brambles on the edge of the water. Quickly he ran back to the gate and back into the field to the ditch. The only way that he could get to the staff was by getting into the ditch. He took off his shoes and socks and rolled up the legs of his short trousers, but the water was so deep that he got the bottom of them wet. The brambles didn't give up their captive without a fight, but Brian eventually became the slightly blooded victor and carried the spoils home.

By the time he got back to the cottage all the girls were up and having their breakfast. As he came in, they all looked at him. It was only then that he became aware how bedraggled his appearance must be. He most certainly looked as if he had been pulled through a hedge backwards because that was more or less what had happened to him. With a great flourish he produced the staff from behind his back. His mum was just about to say 'look at the sight of you' but she was beaten to it by his cry of 'tada!' 'Mary's face was a picture when she saw the staff. As Brian handed it to her he told her where it had been found. Then he pointed out a small area where immersion in the water had made visible a few extra carvings of what appeared to be more Arabic writing.

The news of the reappearance of water in the stream which ran through part of the village spread through Blean like wildfire. Within ten days of the appearance of the water, four acre field was already taking on a green hue and before the middle of September George was using it to graze the cattle. The stream continued to flow despite the fact that the drought was continuing throughout the rest of the country. As a result of this, Blean became famous for a few days. The local newspaper even featured it on its front page: 'Local village saved from drought by mysterious appearance of a spring.' The story said that 'Children playing in a nearby wood disturbed a large stone that was capping a previously unknown spring ...'

After the summer holiday was over, the appearance of the spring became the topic of school conversation for a few days, but none of the children from the cottage mentioned the striking of the stone with the rod. As soon as the rain came in the autumn the whole story was forgotten – but not by Mary. The stream never dried up. Their apparent rural idyllic life continued because George kept his job.

CHAPTER SEVENTEEN

When she was twelve, Mary won a scholarship and went to a grammar school in Canterbury, where she excelled at French, German and History. Later, after outstanding exam results she went on to college to train to be a teacher. She began the course as a 'Recognised Student in Training' a year before the outbreak of World War II. She had been given a grant for the year of training from the Board of Education, in return for a pledge to teach for five years on completion of the course.

During that year of training she lodged with an aunt. Well, Mary called her 'aunt', but in reality she was close friend of her parents: she had left the village of Blean and had gone to live in London shortly after her husband had died. The accommodation was ideal. Mary had a room of her own and travelled the few miles to college each day by bus.

The outbreak of World War II meant that her plans had to be changed. She volunteered to join the WRNS in early 1940 and as a consequence was granted a dispensation that allowed her to postpone the teaching commitment until after the war.

As she stood at the gates of HMS Pembroke at Mill Hill in the borough of Barnet, clutching her small suitcase, she was overawed by the imposing gates of what had once been a hospital. It felt bit like that first day at school when she was five years old.

This was the beginning of a most dramatic period in her life. At the Mill Hill depot she became reacquainted with communal living – although Mary had shared a room with her two sisters at the cottage, this communal living was somewhat different and the way that service life centred upon discipline was a real eye-opener for her.

It was soon to become obvious that the fact that she had been interested in languages from a very young age and had studied German at school and college had been entered in her records. Three weeks after enlisting, she was collected from Mill Hill and taken by naval van to Admiralty House. She was ushered into a large room in which there were about a dozen other Wrens. Gradually they were joined, in dribs and drabs, by another dozen or so who must have come from bases further away. Talking to others in the room, it became apparent that what they had in common was the fact that they had some knowledge of German. After about an hour a naval officer entered and told them that they were going to have their knowledge of spoken German tested. It turned out to be a very thorough and intensive test lasting nearly two hours, after which they were all transported back to their bases.

It was back to HMS Pembroke for Mary, but she stayed there for only a few days before – at short notice – she was transferred. She became familiar with the word 'posted' – *'makes you feel a bit like a parcel,'* she thought – to an Admiralty unit in a large house in Southfield, Wimbledon. She had been successful in the test and was one of those selected for a rigorous, intensive and demanding course in receiving, recording and logging German spoken radio communications. She and the rest of the group – about a dozen in all – were billeted in a nearby large house which, like the main establishment, had been requisitioned by the Admiralty. This was a change from the large dormitories at Mill Hill, and more like the arrangement that she had been used to when she was growing up, but of course the room she had to share with three others in the big house was far grander than the room that she had shared with her sisters at home.

The four-week course included learning the slang and shorthand terms used by the German military in their radio transmissions. They had to learn how to log the translation of the exchanges and how to report them.

It didn't take Mary long to realise that all her fellow Wrens on the course came from rather well-to-do families, but because there was very little free time, she didn't manage to establish friendships with any of them. Most of the rooms in the house where they were billeted had been converted into sleeping quarters. Each of these rooms contained two bunk beds and, as the lower bunk was always the first choice, and as Mary was the last to be allocated to her particular room, she ended up with a top bunk.

At the end of the four weeks everyone passed, and they were given the rank of Acting Petty Officer. When the postings came out Mary discovered that she and Edwina, one of the 'posh' Wrens, had been posted to HMS Daedalus, a Fleet Air Arm Naval station at Lee-on-the-Solent, in Hampshire. So she was on the move once again.

❦

Within a week of their arrival on the base at the end of June, King George VI visited the establishment. One of his ceremonial duties was to review the WRNS: Mary and Edwina were both included among those who were inspected even though they had only been in the King's service for a mere three months. Everything was happening at a whirlwind pace.

Although the posting was to HMS Daedalus, Mary and Edwina were billeted outside the main camp in a large house that had once been a preparatory school for sons of gentlemen, in the tree-lined Manor Way of Lee-on- the Solent. There were over thirty WRNS billeted in this large house, which – like those in Wimbledon – had been requisitioned by the Admiralty, though this time the Wrens were accommodated in small dormitories of six beds.

The place where Mary and Edwina were assigned to carry out their duties was not in the 'camp', but at Seafield Park, about a mile to the west of Daedalus. Every day they were taken there and brought back by truck. On the first day they were joined by another four Wrens and the six of them were to be the day watch. The six who made up the night watch were by then back at the billet in Manor Way, catching up on their sleep. It seemed strange that although they were technically based at Daedalus they spent only about ten percent of their time there. On that first day when they were taken to Seafield, the First Officer Wren (Special Duties) who was in charge showed Mary and Edwina their work stations and gave them a quick rundown on the procedures and duties. Then it was in at the deep end. The First Officer reminded them that they had all signed the official secrets act, and under no circumstances whatsoever were they to talk about or discuss, not even among themselves, the work that they were doing at Seafield Park. Occasionally they had to be present on Daedalus for other duties, but for most of their time they were either at Seafield Park or Manor Way, so they were somewhat separated from the rest of the personnel at Daedalus.

It was six weeks after their arrival, on Friday 16 August, during the day watch, when all hell broke loose. The German wireless transmissions started being detected in such profusion that the 'listeners' were hard-pressed to receive, translate record and log all the communications between the aircraft, as the German aircrews frenziedly and frantically shouted instructions and comments to one another. It became obvious that they were bound for the south coast on a bombing mission. The phones in the listening centre became red hot as fighter command and all potential targets were alerted. The Wrens, although totally focused on the communications that they were intercepting, were also aware of the siren sounding. There was no question of them taking cover in the air raid shelter. They had to remain on duty. Then they heard the noise of the exploding bombs and the sound of gunfire. Although they knew that it was Daedalus that was being hit, it seemed at times as if the attack was taking place directly above their heads. Although the raid seemed to go on forever: in reality it was only for about half an hour. They then started to pick up transmissions indicating that the German aircraft were on their way back to their bases in northern France. Shortly after that, the 'all clear' sounded.

In the evening, when they were being taken back to their billet, everyone in the truck was completely silent, which was very unusual. As the transport made its way along Marine

Parade, the road that ran along the seafront at Lee-on-the-Solent, they could see and smell evidence of the raid. Smoke was still weaving its way out of the damaged and destroyed hangars. Twisted piles of metal that had once been aircraft were littered across the airfield. It was just coming up to high tide, there was no wind, the sun was low down on the horizon casting a shimmering ribbon of orange light on the glass like surface of the Solent: a totally idyllic scene on one side, but evidence of carnage and destruction on the other. For some reason it made Mary think of 'paradise lost and paradise regained' but this remained an unspoken thought. The atmosphere in the billet that evening was very subdued. Later that night, just before lights out, the First Officer came into the dormitory of the day watch.

'Stand easy. Sit on your beds, ladies, if you wish,' she said. 'What we have been through today shows you how important your work is. Without your efforts today many more would have been killed. Well done. Try to put it out of your minds for a while and try to get a good night's sleep. Good night and thank you all. Don't bother to get up when I go out.'

There was a chorus of voices as she turned and left: 'thank you, ma'am, Goodnight.'

Next day it was back to work as usual, but now they were all different people. Gradually the horrific events of that Friday began to be pushed to the backs of their minds. Two days later there was another period of frenzied activity for the now seasoned 'signals interceptors', but on this occasion the targets were concentrated over Kent and the counties on the east coast. This time the action lasted almost two hours, but after these bombing raids and the ensuing dogfights there was a period of relative calm. A month later on the Saturday night of 14 September, Mary and Edwina decided on the spur of the moment to go to the dance at the Tower ballroom just a half-mile walk away on the seafront.

The dancehall was packed with young and a few not so young sailors anxious for a bit of 'female company' – the Wrens had been warned about this and its possible consequences in the first three weeks of their training. Mary, having grown up on a farm, was well aware about certain aspects of the warning talk. Although Edwina had attended the same lecture, Mary could sense that she had not fully understood some of it, and when she explained certain aspects to her, Edwina was quite shocked. Not quite as shocked as she might have been if she had not been forewarned.

They had no shortage of dance partners, and each and every one of those with whom they danced asked – unsuccessfully – if they could 'accompany' them back to their billet after the dance. Despite the numerous posters pointing out 'Dangerous talk costs lives', some of the young Fleet Air Arm men talked about what they did. One particular young chap told her that he had been lucky to get a forty-eight hour pass – probably trying to indicate that he didn't have to be back on board by 23:59. Then, trying to impress even more, he added that his Chief, Jack Toulson, was so pleased with his work that he was the only one chosen for the pass. He might have thought that it was going to be his lucky night when the attractive Wren responded to him, and continued the conversation by asking him what his Chief looked like. The description left her in no doubt that this was her uncle Jack, especially the young mechanic's comment: 'he's got blue eyes that look right into you'.

A little later, about a quarter to ten, Mary and Edwina left the dance and made their way back to the billet to get there before lights out. It never was going to be the young airframe mechanic's lucky day, or his lucky night.

Mary had only been detailed on half-a-dozen occasions for duties on the main base of Daedalus, including the auspicious time when King George VI conducted a review. But as soon as she could, and that was over a week later, she managed to get herself sent there on some trivial errand. On this particular visit she began to realise how many Wrens there were on the base. *'Good job I'm not a German spy,'* she thought as she made her way unchallenged around the various aircraft hangers.

Then she had a stroke of luck – she spotted the young mechanic who had told her about Jack. More accurately, he caught sight of Mary and called out 'can I help you, miss?' He was probably fantasising that she had come to see him. She turned and walked towards him smiling; his concupiscence changed up a gear.

'Can you tell me where I might find Chief Petty Officer Toulson?'

His concupiscence withered and his lust bit the dust. He looked a bit worried – perhaps he thought she had come to report him for talking about his work on the base.

'He's over there in that hanger, checking on one of the Swordfishes,' he said, cautiously nodding to a hangar just off to her left.

She thanked him again with a smile and made her way over to the hangar. Near its entrance she could make out a group of young men being given what appeared to be a dressing-down by someone that she immediately recognised. It was indeed 'Uncle Jack'. When he'd finished 'talking' to the group she walked over to him, aware as she did so of how – in her brief time in the WRNS – the way that she walked had changed. Now it was more of a march than a walk. Jack looked up as she approached. At first he thought she was a Wren from one of the other hangars where some were being trained in aircraft repairs.

'Hello Chief, I'm Mary – you used to come and visit us at Blean before the war.'

'Good grief, Mary, I would never have known you, you're so ... so grown up. I haven't seen you since you were ... what was it? Ten years old. You're looking really good.'

The young mechanics looked on enviously.

'Look, Mary – Margaret and me live in Lee with our kids. We must make arrangements for you to come and have a meal with us.'

Jack took a pencil out of the top pocket of his overalls and wrote down the address on the back of a cigarette packet. They talked for a little while longer, but it was a somewhat difficult time for Jack because there was a bit of a rush on for a particular job. Actually it was one hell of a rush. Mary told Jack that she could get time off on the next-but-one Sunday – 6 October – and so it was agreed. She would go to Sunday lunch with them on that day.

When he went back into the hangar one of the lusty young mechanics called out: 'What have you got that we don't have, Chief?'

'Apart from charm, good looks, intelligent conversation and these three buttons, nothing at all,' he said. 'Now get on with the jobs I've given you. Nobody goes off duty until this old Stringbag is fighting fit and airworthy, and don't forget what I said about those wing struts.'

Jack never forgot the time in that Ninack at Abu Seuir, seeing that tension wire slacken and the strut dramatically breaking. Ever since that crash Jack, who had always been careful and thorough with aircraft maintenance, had become religiously meticulous with each and every strut and tension wire procedure.

CHAPTER EIGHTEEN

On the Sunday, Mary arrived at Jack's house – about a mile from her billet in Manor Way – exactly on time. She had always been one for punctuality. She had a very enjoyable lunch with Jack and Margaret and was delighted to discover that they had two children: nine-year-old Tom, whose birthday was the same date as Mary's, and five-year-old Teresa.

It's strange how we remember in some detail trivial happenings in our lives; so it was with Mary and the meal of roast leg of lamb that she had on that day. It was a memory that she would carry with her for many years.

There was so much to chat about. First, Jack explained how he had been posted to Cranwell then to RAF Lee-on-the-Solent, where he had transferred from the RAF to the Fleet Air Arm a few months before the outbreak of the war. Mary told them that her mum and dad were doing well, and how she was halfway to being a teacher and would take up teaching after the war. Her brother Brian had joined up and was in the RAF training as aircrew to be an Observer. Alice and Eileen were both training to be nurses. At one time she talked about the 'staff' that Uncle Jack had given her and the mystical event when the spring and stream had appeared on the farm. She said that Brian couldn't remember where he had put the rattling stone. On hearing this, possibly just to show that boys could be trusted to remember where they put things, Tom nipped out to the shed and brought in the orangey brown stone that his dad had given him, similar to the one that they had been talking about. Tom, like all the others who came into possession of any of these stones, had very quickly lost interest in it.

'That certainly brings back memories, Uncle Jack,' Mary said, as they each took a turn at the almost compulsory ritual of rattling it.

Margaret had made some jam tarts and scones, which they all tucked into at tea-time before Mary had to say farewell and make her way back to the billet. Before she left she assured Margaret and Jack that she would let her mum and dad know that she had been to see them and pass on all of their news.

Over the next two months, time in its perfidious cloak of regularity conspired with events to ensure that Mary only managed to have brief conversations with Jack on three occasions.

※

Just after Christmas, completely out of the blue, Mary was posted to HMS *Paragon* – a shore base near Scarborough. As if this wasn't surprise enough, she was also promoted to Acting Third Officer. This meant not only a change of uniform, but a change of duties and responsibilities too. Her experiences during the attack on HMS *Daedalus* had given her an insight into the purposes and importance of the tasks of Special Duties personnel. She was placed in charge of two watches of what appeared to be very young Wrens, although four of her 'charges' were in fact older than she was. Her promotion to officer status meant that she was now billeted out to establishments where she would have a room to herself. These were former summer lodging houses which, although they had not been not requisitioned by the military, were reserved for service personnel, mainly officers in the WRNS. Mary considered herself very lucky because she was allocated a room in a lodging house in Foreshore Road, which even had a sea view.

Scarborough reminded her a little of Ramsgate and Margate. She had very pleasant memories of both of these towns from the occasional family day trips that they had made when she was young, and which now seemed as if they were a lifetime away. Scarborough was a very pretty and pleasant place in the summer, but this was not summer, it was mid-winter and it was cold – especially when the wind blew in from the North Sea, as it seemed to do most of the time.

Following the attack on *Daedalus*, and the large-scale raid on the east coast two days afterwards, the pace of activity at Seafield Park had slowed. Mary was soon to realise why she had been posted to the north east coast: the German offensive was now beginning to increasingly target parts of the industrial north. These offensives consisted of waves of squadrons of bombers coming in across the North Sea. She and her watches were part of a much bigger op's room at a Wireless Telegraphy station a few miles from HMS *Paragon*. Although the conversations that they would pick up were never as frantic as those she experienced on her initiation, they were – unknown to the German aircrews – often quite revealing and this was very helpful in directing the fighter squadrons based at the many aerodromes in the surrounding area. One of the advantages of operating near Scarborough was that it was never a main target of the bombers.

Just forty miles south of HMS *Paragon* was HMS *Beaver* – a pretentious name for a Godforsaken tiny W/T base at Withernsea. There the 'listeners' were only about ten miles from Hull, which was frequently the target, and they could hear the exploding bombs in the same way that Mary had experienced when Daedalus was raided. Mary was quite pleased that she was only required on a couple of dozen occasions to take charge of the watches at HMS *Beaver*.

The summers at Scarborough proved to be a great deal more pleasant and Mary remained at HMS *Paragon* for over three years. She was delighted when, in 1944, she was posted back to HMS *Daedalus* together with a promotion to Second Officer. The activities at Seafield Park were very much concentrated on the D-Day invasion. The 'listeners' in this case were able pass on information to the allied command centre about what the Germans knew – or didn't know – about what was going on.

During the summer of 1943 Mary and her family back at Blean had been informed that Brian had been shot down and was a prisoner of war. After that, whenever she was on watch, she would often visualise young German women in W/T stations performing similar functions to those of her 'charges', listening to the radio communications between the aircrew members on British aircraft.

Not long after VE Day, which coincidently was George's fiftieth birthday, Mary was demobbed. It seemed so strange and the thought of not having to go back to any naval or RAF base left Mary with very mixed feelings. She was pleased that her experiences of the war were all behind her, but it was tempered by the realisation that she would be unlikely to ever see again many of the friends that she'd made during the past five years.

※

The most vivid impression she had as she walked into the cottage was how small it was – it was as if time had shrunk it – but then she realised that it was only a trick of memory as she recalled how the three girls had only just managed to fit into the one bedroom when they were all at home. Her parents were still the same cheery people that Mary remembered, but they were different in an indefinable way, not just because both of them now had mostly grey hair, and her dad was beginning to go a bit thin on top; it was the way they talked and looked at their now grown-up children. They were so proud of them all and pleased that they had all survived the war, although it was more than a month before Brian was repatriated. When he arrived home he looked very gaunt and haggard but he still had the same smile that they all recognised.

In the September of 1945 Mary was directed to a teaching post in a school in south London and resumed her teaching career. Within a year her leadership qualities were recognised and she was appointed deputy head of the language department. Although she was only the deputy, in reality by the end of that year she was the one who was running the show. Mary had a very good working relationship with the head of the department who was approaching the end of her career and who was more than pleased to have Mary running the department. On her retirement, the post of head of the language department was offered to Mary, and much to the surprise of everyone including the headmaster – especially the headmaster – Mary declined the offer. There had been some confusion and his secretary had failed to let him know that Mary had given in her notice. She had now completed the requirement for the Recognised Student in Training and had decided to look elsewhere.

When she was based at HMS *Daedalus* she had fallen in love with the area, and decided that she would like to live in that part of the country. Consequently she had applied for the post of head of the language department at an independent school for girls in Southsea that she had seen advertised in the *Times Educational Supplement*. The interview had gone like a dream. One of the Board of Governors had formerly held a senior post in the WRNS, and the Headmistress – who had a mind like a filing cabinet – took to Mary because they were very like-minded and hit it off immediately. She was offered the post the same day, and promptly accepted it.

When the schools broke up for the summer holidays in 1950, and Mary's time at the school in London came to an end, she said goodbye to the rest of the staff, and this took quite a while because she had made many good friends during her five-year stay. It was then back to the basement flat that she had been renting for all the time that he had been teaching at the school. Although she had paid her rent up to the end of the month, she let the landlord know that she would vacate the flat before then. The day after the school broke up she made her way home to Blean.

Although she was concerned about the extra number of 'things' that she had accumulated over the past five years, and would be bringing home to her family's cramped cottage, it proved not to be a problem. The year before, her younger sister Alice had married a doctor at the hospital where she had been working and they had set up home in Ashford, where her husband had had become a GP under the new NHS scheme. This meant that there would only be two of them to share the small bedroom. At least, that is what Mary thought. When she arrived home she discovered that in fact she would have the room all to herself because Eileen had joined the RAF as a Nursing Sister and wouldn't be home until Christmas.

Brian was working as a draughtsman at an engineering company in Canterbury.

'He's courting a young lady who's a secretary in the front office of the company – wouldn't be surprised if they don't get engaged soon. We don't see so much of him lately,' said her mum, in a voice tinged with regret, as they sat in the kitchen chatting on Mary's first day at home. The cottage was very much quieter, unlike the old days when there was always something going on. Of course there had been the usual arguments, but for the most part, it had been a very happy household. Mary put a consoling arm around her mum. She didn't need to say anything.

The next day she decided to give her mother a surprise treat, so on the spur of the moment she said: 'C'mon Mum let's go a catch a bus'.

Esme started to give reasons why she couldn't, but Mary would have none of it. The two of them made a trip into Ramsgate to join the holiday-makers. They strolled along the Marina Esplanade and watched the kiddies being given rides along the sands on donkeys. This reminded Mary of the donkey rides that she and her brother and sisters had had on the same patch when they were young. Then they bought cockles from the one of the stalls near the 'Pav'; they even had some candy floss. It was then across the road to the rock factory to watch at the window at the front, as the large lump was progressively rolled and pulled into thinner and thinner forms, gradually being reduced in size, with the name Ramsgate running right through its middle. They bought a large bag of rock to take home.

'Mum – this brings back memories. Do you remember that time when Uncle Jack brought a large bag of rock to the cottage, the time when he gave me that 'stick'? I loved that old piece of wood – I really thought it had magical powers. Do you know what became of it?'

'Yes, dear. I put it at the back of that cupboard near the kitchen stove where I put the bed linen to air. I also found the rattling stone Brian had lost and put it with the stick.'

It was one of the best days that both of them could remember in a long, long time. For Esme it was almost as good as that day when she'd received the telegram informing the family that Brian was alive and a prisoner of war, three months after she'd received the first one telling them that Brian had been posted as missing in action. It had been a limbo of grief between the two telegrams.

They arrived back at Blean both with radiant faces, shining not just because they had been in the sun but glowing mainly with sheer inner pleasure.

The next day, Mary said to her mum: 'While I still think about it, I'll rummage out that old stick and the rattling stone, and take them over to the Powell Cotton museum at Birchington on the Margate road. I believe they collect African artefacts. Possibly they would like them.'

So after breakfast she borrowed her mum's bike and cycled into Whitstable where she caught a train to Birchington. She had wrapped the 'staff' in newspaper; the stone fitted easily into the pocket of the cardigan that she was wearing. Travelling in the guard's van with the bike was not too bad as it was only a short journey, less than fifteen miles and just three stops. It took less than half an hour to get to her destination. In the guard's van she sat on one of the hampers of oysters which were on their way to hotels in Margate and Ramsgate. After she got off the train it was just over a mile to the museum. Unfortunately, although she arrived there before eleven, no-one was available to see her until after one o'clock.

The curator's assistant apologised to Mary when she eventually appeared.

'We've had a bit of a rush on this morning because the curator has decided to completely change one of the displays,' she said. She paused to catch her breath, and then asked 'How can I help you?'

'Would these be of interest to the museum?' Mary said, as she held out the rattling stone, the stick with the carved Arabic script, and the partial writing on the paper-like material for the assistant to have a look at.

The assistant's eyes lit up when she saw the Arabic carving and script.

'That's parchment,' she said, pointing to the paper-like material, 'and at a guess I would say it was made from goat's skin. It could easily be a thousand years old. I am studying Arabic but the only word that I can recognise is 'Queen'. Oh and there, near the bottom of the stick I think that word could be 'Massa'. I've recently been reading about that area.'

Mary hadn't noticed the fainter carving near the bottom before. It was the newspaper print that had made it visible. Then she remembered her brother Brian mentioning something about it when he found it for her, the day after she had lost it up in the woods above four acre field.

Before the curator's assistant had chance to comment on the stone Mary said 'shake it'.

'Ah! One of my colleagues is interested in geology – I'm sure that he would be interested in that, she said.

Mary told how the artefacts had come into her possession and what her Uncle Jack had said about them. She didn't mention the mysterious spring at Blean. The curator's assistant went on to say that the museum would be interested in researching and displaying them, but she added that Mary would have to sign a standard form to the effect that they were hers and she was donating them to the museum and thereby relinquishing all ownership rights. They talked for a further quarter of an hour, after which Mary started her return journey back to Blean. As she came out of the park grounds where the museum was located, a plane came into land at Manston. It was only then that she realised how close the museum was to where Uncle Jack had been based all those years ago.

The next two weeks passed pleasurably and not too rapidly, but eventually it was time for her to make her way to Southsea. The first task on her arrival was to make arrangements for a place to stay. Despite the fact that it was still summer and nearly all the boarding houses were proudly wearing their 'No Vacancies' boards, she had been able to book a week in a B&B. This gave her plenty of time to sort out her future accommodation. Fortunately, finding suitable lodgings was not to prove to be too much of a problem. The school had an arrangement with a number of boarding houses in the nearby area, which was a little way back from the seafront. The proprietors of these establishments were quite keen to offer accommodation to the lady members of the staff because it meant that they would have the rooms occupied all year round. Also they were well aware that their teacher tenants would have been carefully vetted by the prestigious school. Mary chose the second room that she viewed, possibly because the landlady reminded her of her mum, possibly because the room had a sunnier aspect. Whichever it was, this was to become her home for the foreseeable future. It was ideal, as it was less than a five minutes' walk to the school and about the same distance to a selection of 'quality' shops.

Mary settled into the school and life took on a new order.

CHAPTER NINETEEN

The second of June 1953 was to be a Tuesday that Esme would never forget. Like so many throughout the country, she had managed to get herself invited into the home of one of the neighbours who had one of these 'new fangled' television sets, the presence of which was advertised by the H-shaped aerial strapped to the chimney. The house that Esme went to was a detached property on the corner of the main road to Whitstable. Needless to say, the family that lived there was rather well-off. There were only two households that boasted a TV set in the whole of the village. It seemed that everyone who had not been able to go to London to line the streets had gathered around television sets throughout the land to watch the blurred, often flickering, images of the coronation of Queen Elizabeth II at Westminster Abbey. Many husbands who were, by the nature of things, the sole operators of the 'cutting edge' technological apparatus had their abilities frequently questioned that day as they frantically adjusted the brightness and contrast controls, and more critically the vertical and horizontal hold control buttons at the back of the TV receivers.

Fifteen people had crammed into the front room of the house where Esme was, and all were sitting open-mouthed in awe at the spectacle unfolding before them. The crown was just being held above the head of the new queen when there was a knock on the front door of the house.

'Who the Dickens can that be?' the lady of the house exclaimed, with more than a hint of annoyance in her voice as she made her way to the door. It turned out to be the village bobby.

'Could I have a word with Esme, please ma'am?'

The look on the constable's face sent her hurrying back into the front room.

'The constable wants to have a word with you, Esme.'

Squeezing past the bodies in the room, Esme's heart was beating sixteen to the dozen. When she got to the front door, with a shaky voice she asked: 'What is it, Albert?'

'Maybe we'd better talk about it down at the station, Es.'

The Police Station was an end-of-terrace house, just six doors down, with a counter in the front room that served as the front desk. Albert was the sole occupant of this outpost of law and order. Esme grabbed her coat from the pile on the stairs and made her way to the station with him. It had stopped raining at last.

When they reached the station the constable said to her: 'Just take a seat over there, Es and I will go and make a nice cup of tea.'

How long does it take to make a cup of tea? If you had asked Esme at that time she would have said an eternity. But, after a few minutes Albert came back into the 'office' with two enamel mugs of tea. He had put at least four spoons of sugar in Esme's mug.

After she had taken a few sips of the sweet tea, Albert looked closely at her.

'There's been an accident, Es. George's tractor rolled over with him on board.'

The constable watched as the colour drained from her face, until it became the same colour as the white in the red white and blue bunting that was decorating the office and which seemed so inappropriate for the present situation.

'Is he ..?'

'I'm so sorry, Es – he didn't make it.'

Albert just managed to grab the mug and prevent it falling to the floor.

Although the police constable was someone who tended

to avoid any physical contact, he sat alongside Esme and put his arm around her shoulder, to comfort and support her. Albert had known George and Esme for almost seven years, and had spoken to them almost every day during that period. Although his position required that he shouldn't be too friendly with anyone within his area of responsibility, he had without doubt become their friend and they had become his. He was a big man as was befitting of an officer of the law, with a normally stern face which he kept for display when he was on his beat. He wasn't married. He had been 'walking out' with a young lady for more than two years, and everyone assumed they would get married, but the war intervened. When he was called-up and had gone off to fight for his country, she had told him of her undying love and how she would wait for him. The reality was that she only waited until the Yanks arrived. Whether it was the attraction of the uniform or the nylons with which she had been plied, the outcome was that she ended up 'in trouble', eventually becoming a war bride. She left for America with her infant just one week before Albert arrived home. She didn't even leave a note to explain what had happened; she just left. Albert had been heartbroken, his mother was very bitter indeed and when a few years later she learned that the young lady's life had gone right off the rails, with two more children and a husband who had moved on to pastures new, her only comment was that it 'served the little cow right'. Albert, though not quite so vindictive, resigned himself to being a lifelong bachelor. Ever since he arrived in the village a year after the end of the war, Esme George and their children had become a surrogate family for him, despite the fact most of the children by then had flown the nest.

'Look, Es – you will need someone with you. If you give me Alice's address in Ashford I'll phone the station there and they will send someone round to let her know what has happened.'

An hour later Alice and her doctor husband pulled up in their car outside. Almost before it had come to a halt, Alice jumped out of the car and ran into the police station. Albert had already completed a series of procedures, almost as if this was an everyday event, but the truth of it was that this was only the third occasion in all his time at Blean that he had had to deal with an unexpected death. The coroner had been informed, a police sergeant had arrived from Canterbury and the undertaker had been summoned. Alice just went and hugged her mum and they spent the next ten minutes crying their eyes out. The doctor, because of the nature of his work, had often come across grieving families, but this time it was his own. He went out his car to fetch his medical bag and administered a sedative to Esme and Alice. Half an hour later the three of them left the police station, got into his almost brand new Triumph Mayflower and set off for the cottage. Albert began sorting out the necessary paperwork, before making his way to the farm and the scene of the accident. As Esme got into the car, through her red-rimmed watery eyes, tried a smile and said: 'This is a very nice car, Peter.'

'Thank you, Mum – let's get you home.'

Esme had always liked the fact that right from the day that he had married Alice, he had always called her Mum.

Before he had left his surgery Peter had made calls to Mary's lodging house in Southsea and to Brian's work place in Canterbury. He had been unable to get a message to Eileen because she was serving abroad with the RAF in Aden. When they got to the cottage, a great deal of activity was going on down by the Dutch barn. Esme wanted to go down to see George but Peter persuaded her that it would not be a good idea until the police had sorted everything out.

'When they've done what they have to do, they'll let you know and tell you when it will be possible for you to go and see him,' he said. 'It's most likely they'll suggest that you wait until he is being taken care of by the undertakers.'

From his past experience Peter knew that this would take quite a while, so he led them all into the cottage. He then suggested the universal panacea:

'Let's all have a nice cup of tea.'

Of course the cottage had all its unfortunate reminders of George. His coat was hung behind the kitchen door, his spare boots neatly placed in the corner, his shirts carefully folded on the dresser.

'He's such a tidy person,' said Esme, then with an inward look added, 'he was'.

She had temporarily run out of tears.

Shortly after they all entered the cottage Albert arrived back at the scene of the accident, reporting to the sergeant who had come over from Canterbury. The sergeant was satisfied that everything that needed to be done had been done. Statements had been taken from the two farm labourers who had witnessed the tractor rolling over, and a report had been compiled. Not long after this, the undertaker arrived and George's body was handed over to him. He and his team took charge of George's remains and set about transferring them to the mortuary.

Brian arrived at the cottage just after six o'clock, but Mary not until nearly 10 o'clock, just as it was just getting dark. The festive crowds in London had meant that it had taken her a lot longer to make travel connections.

When she arrived, at first she thought that no-one was at home because the cottage was in darkness. She tried the latch – it was undone. As she walked in she was just able to make out the four figures inside in the gloom. This was not the time for words. She walked across and just hugged and cried with her mum, in the same way that Alice had done. After a few minutes she dried her eyes, her organisational instincts took charge and she broke the silence.

'Peter, perhaps you could take Brian home to his wife while Alice and I get Mum off to bed and then we can work out what to do in the morning,' she said.

And that is what happened. When Peter got back, Alice and Mary had managed to get Esme into bed and had organised the rest of the sleeping arrangements. Peter and Alice were to have Brian's old room and Mary had the room she had occupied for a little while three years ago. That night Hypnos and Morpheus were very tardy in arriving, and it was well into the small hours before all in the cottage had managed to get to sleep. The dreams that Morpheus brought that night were all of a sleep-disturbing nature which did not help at all. It was already light by five o'clock when, un-refreshed, the household began to stir to cope with the realities of the day.

Mary went into the village and sent a telegram to Eileen to let her know about her dad's accident. By lunchtime arrangements had been made for the funeral on Thursday 11

June. Brian together with his wife Rose had been collected from Canterbury, and a family meeting was convened in the kitchen. It only seemed natural that Mary should take charge, which of course she did. After she had summarised what had been done, including the arrangement to go and see Dad's body at the undertakers, she turned to what was going to be the most pressing problem. As the cottage which had been home for the past thirty-four years was a 'tied' property it meant that in the very near future Esme would have no home.

'Look Mum, the farmer is going to want the cottage for a new stockman so we will have to think about where you are going to live,' she said.

Almost in unison Brian, Rose, Alice and Peter said: 'she can come and live with us'. Mary smiled and looked at Alice and Rose.

'Do you two want to tell us anything?' she asked.

They both looked at each other as if to say 'how on earth did she know?' and then back at Mary. Alice was the first to speak.

'I don't know how you knew, Mary, because Peter and I haven't told a soul, but we are expecting a baby'.

Then it was Rose's turn. 'It's the same for us, we're also expecting a baby.'

There was quite a babble of conversation for a minute. It turned out that both babies were due about Christmas time.

Mary brought the family meeting back to matters in hand.

'Well, Mum, it looks like you're going to be a granny twice over before the end of the year.' It was good to see her mum smiling in the middle of such a bad time. 'Why I asked about Alice and Rose's condition was because, although it is very nice of them both to offer to let you live with them, when the babies arrive it will be very difficult.'

'But I would be able to help with the babies,' interrupted Esme.

'I know that you would, Mum, and they both would love it, but neither of them have enough rooms for it to be practical.' Mary paused before continuing: she knew the pause would concentrate their minds. 'How about if I look for a bigger flat in Southsea so that Mum comes to live with me? There are lots of nice shops, cinemas and parks nearby.'

The discussion continued for a little while. Eventually everyone agreed that Mary's solution was the best.

As an interim measure, it was decided that it would not be a good idea for Mum to be left on her own at the cottage, so a bag was packed for her and she stayed with Brian and Rose until after the funeral. When Esme moved out of the cottage she would live with Alice and Peter until Mary arranged for the accommodation in Southsea.

After they had all been to the undertakers to say goodbye to Dad, Esme was taken to the two-up two-down that Brian and Rose rented in Canterbury. Mary made her way back to Southsea.

Two days later, on the Saturday, she caught the trolley bus to the harbour and took a ferry across to Gosport and then a bus to Lee-on-the-Solent. It was more than ten years since she had visited Uncle Jack and she fully expected that he and his family would have moved to a new address; nevertheless she decided to go to his old address to see if the present occupants knew where he might have moved to. She knocked on the door and a teenage girl answered.

'I'm sorry to disturb you, but do your mum and dad have a forwarding address for Mr Jack Toulson who used to live here?'

The young girl smiled. 'That's my dad – we still live here.'

A voice from the back called out. 'Who is it, Teresa?'

'It's a lady to see you, Dad.'

Jack came through from the kitchen into the hall, saw Mary through the open front door and recognised her immediately.

'Come in, Mary, come in.' Turning to Teresa he said: 'Mum's in the back garden – go and tell her that we've got a guest. Tell her that Mary's here, there's a good girl.'

As Teresa ran out through the kitchen, Jack showed Mary into the front room, which was exactly as she remembered it. After the usual formality of 'I'll just put the kettle on,' followed by the production of cups of tea together with jam tarts and scones, there was quite a cacophony of chatter because there was so much to catch up with. There were, of course, the profuse apologies about not keeping in touch. After he had said it, Jack wished that he had waited just a little longer before asking how

George was.

'I'm sad to have to tell you, Uncle Jack, but Dad died in a farm accident last Tuesday.'

'Oh, no – I'm so sorry to hear that,' said Jack. 'How is your mum coping? Your dad was a good bloke – you don't need me to tell you that. He and your mum raised a family to be proud of in very difficult times, and under difficult circumstances. I am so pleased that our paths crossed – but it seems incredible that I've known him – sorry … knew him – for over thirty years. You must have heard a hundred times how we met on a train all those years ago. We got on so well. I'm so sorry that I didn't keep in touch with your dad and mum as much as I should've. It must be a very difficult time for you all.'

Mary went on to explain how the family were rallying round. She told Jack that the funeral was to be on the following Thursday at the little church in Blean. Before she could say any more, Jack chipped in.

'I'll be there – what time will it be?'

Mary's face brightened, because this was what she had hoped to hear. Although the two families had drifted apart, Uncle Jack's name came up so often in conversations that it was almost as if he was one of the family. During the previous ten years or so, getting in touch had been one of those things which was always going to be done, but somehow always got put off to another time. Now it was too late for her Dad.

The chatting went on for quite a while. Jack and Margaret were surprised to learn that Mary had been teaching in Southsea for nearly three years. When she told them that her Mum was going to come and live with her in the next few months, they insisted that she must bring her over to see them.

'We really mustn't lose contact with each other again. Now you promise?'

She did, and they didn't, well – not for many years.

Jack and his family had not moved away because after he was demobbed he had managed to get a job working as a civilian employee in HMS *Daedalus*, in a similar role to that which he'd had when he was in the Fleet Air Arm. Getting a compassionate day off work would be no difficulty. After being demobbed at the end of the war, his demob suit had hardly had an airing. Fortunately it was a dark colour and with a white shirt and black tie, it looked quite respectful for the funeral.

'Jack, will you please apologies to Esme and her family for me?' said Margaret on the day that Jack set off for Blean. 'Explain why I couldn't come with you, as much as I would have liked to. Teresa has to have one of us with her when she goes for that interview.'

The weather was fine and warm on that Thursday, but there were less than two dozen people who attended the service. Funerals are always a sombre time, but George's was particularly poignant. Esme had no living relatives other than her children. Her mother and father had died before World War II, she never had any sisters, and her two brothers had been killed in a mine disaster just after the war. George's parents were also dead, and his only surviving relative – a brother – who lived in Middlesbrough, was infirm and unable to travel. They were all pleased that Eileen had been flown home from Aden. It was quite clear from the congregation for his funeral that George and Esme had lived for each other and their children. After the interment in the small graveyard most of the mourners made their way back to the cottage. Fortunately it was dry and sunny, because there was no way they could all have fitted into the little kitchen. Mary had organised all the available chairs to be placed in the sunny parts of the back garden; she had even got Brian and Peter to go down to the barn and get half a dozen bales of straw so that people could use them to sit on. In the morning, before the service, Mary had persuaded her mum to make some small cakes and sandwiches – this was to take her mind off the funeral.

When they got back to the cottage, Jack was one of the first to have a consoling conversation with Esme. Several times while they were talking he was mentally transported back to the first time that he had met George and Esme on that train over thirty years before. She, understandably, was wearing the same worried face that he had seen on that first meeting.

'I'm going to miss this cottage with all of its memories good and bad,' she said. 'Did Mary tell you that I'm going to go and live with her in Southsea, where there are lots of nice shops?'

It was at this point that Jack saw Esme's face take on that look of pleasure which she had shown on the train when mentioning the fact that George's job had a cottage to go with it.

'She did, Esme, and that also means that you will be able to come and visit us.'

Once again her face took on a less haggard look.

Jack really enjoyed catching up with all that had happened to Esme and her family, but a conversation he had later that afternoon was to prove to be the most intriguing he had ever had. Shortly after his chat with Esme, he went and sat on one of the straw bales, and Eileen came and sat alongside him. After they had been talking for a while about the past, she started to tell him about her life in the RAF and in particular about her life at Aden.

'Mary told us kids when we were young how you had taken a photograph of something that wasn't there when you were in Aden. Well, here's something weird that happened to me only a few months ago'.

She then went on to relate how she, together with two other nursing sisters, had gone out on a day off in a Jeep with a female corporal as driver.

'I remembered hearing about how you found that stick and the rattling stones just to the south of Marib, and I told a couple of my colleagues in the hospital about it, and we decided to go and have a look at the place for ourselves,' she said. 'It didn't look to be very far on the map. Well, although those Jeeps can get a fair old lick on, and the fact that we left early in morning, it was after midday before we got there. It can't have changed very much because I could recognise the building from the descriptions that I had heard. There were still some of those orangey ball-shaped stones scattered around. We tried shaking quite a few but could only find one that rattled – one of the other Sisters found it, so she kept it. Now here's where the weird bit comes in. After we had a picnic lunch we decided to take some pictures of us as a group, with the old building in the background. Using my camera, we each took it in turn to take a photo of the others in the group. The driver took the first one, I took the second then the other two took photos in turn.

A few days later I had the film developed. Well like you, Uncle Jack, I discovered that I had taken a photograph of something that wasn't there. Instead of a photo of the others in the group, my shot showed an out of focus picture of what appeared to be an elderly female – I would say a 'bejewelled dignitary' – sitting on a camel. We hadn't seen a camel for at least twenty miles.'

After she had finished telling her tale Jack said: 'When I mentioned that I had taken a picture of something that wasn't there – what was it, nearly thirty year ago? – I was told that it must have been some sort of mirage effect, but I was not convinced. What made it spookier for me was the total lack of noise just at the instant that I took the picture. It was as if the surrounding area had swallowed the voice of the camera and all other noises with it.'

Eileen looked at him wide-eyed.

'That's exactly it, the lack of sound,' she said. 'Like you, I'm absolutely certain my picture wasn't a mirage effect either.'

Their conversation continued for a little while. Eileen said that she would have another chat with him later, before excusing herself to go and have a few words with her brother and brother-in-law. Unfortunately they never got round to having a second chat. After she went to find them, Albert, the village bobby – who was not in uniform – came up sat alongside Jack and introduced himself.

'You must be the famous Uncle Jack,' he said. 'Pleased to meet you. George and Es were always talking about you and the young chap who committed suicide.'

Albert and Jack sat and chatted for over a quarter of an hour.

It was getting on towards four o'clock when Peter offered to give Jack a lift into Canterbury so that he could catch a train to London. When he arrived home, Margaret had some good news: Teresa had been successful in her interview and would be starting a job at the bank in the High Street in September after her sixteenth birthday.

CHAPTER TWENTY

Mary's plan worked perfectly – she managed to rent a two-bedroom flat just a few doors from the apartment that she had called home for the past three years. It suited the needs of both her mum and herself. On the first of September Esme moved into what was to be her home for almost the next thirty years and Mary became the fourth member of staff at the school to become a 'spinster lady caring for her mother'. In fact these members of staff formed a small club that met up once a month, mainly to go to local tea-shops for tea and chat. Sometimes they went to the cinema or a show at South Parade Pier. Needless to say the club was Mary's idea, and it was quite helpful in enabling Esme to settle into her new environment. The two of them together made regular trips every few months or so across the ferry to Gosport to visit Jack and Margaret in Lee-on-the-Solent.

The Christmas of Esme's first year in Southsea turned out to be a time of great excitement. Both Rose and Alice had their babies on Christmas Eve, Rose in Canterbury Hospital maternity ward, and Alice's at home – despite her husband being a doctor, they hadn't left enough time to get to the hospital. Both of the babies were boys Alice's son was called George after his grandfather, which pleased Esme immensely.

During the summer of their third year in Southsea, on one of their visits to Lee-on-the-Solent, they met Jack and Margaret's son Tom. He was now twenty-four years old, a scaled-down version of his dad but without those penetrating eyes. He worked in a factory in Gosport that made radios and televisions. Mary learnt that he spent all his spare time attending night classes at the Municipal College in Portsmouth. Both he and his sister Teresa got married the year after this meeting. Esme and Mary were invited to both weddings, and on each occasion it was a real trip down memory lane for Mary because the wedding receptions were held in the restaurant at Lee Tower. The next time Mary met Tom was in a totally unexpected situation. It happened eleven year later, in 1968.

The physics teacher at Mary's school, who was married to a naval officer, had informed Miss Bramble that she would be leaving at the end of the summer term to have a baby. The headmistress had an advertisement placed in the *Times Educational Supplement* for a physics teacher, but there were only three applicants and one of them was a man. Much to the utter amazement of everyone in the school, the man was offered the job; and to Mary's astonishment, it turned out to be Tom. After sixteen years in the electronics industry, he had decided to change careers and had just completed his course at the teacher training college in Portsmouth.

Miss Bramble was ignoring the tradition of the school, which had never had a male teacher in its ninety-year history. Many of the lady teachers asked the Headmistress:

'What will the parents of our girls think about us having a male teacher?'

'He's a married man with a ten-year-old daughter,' she replied in a tone which indicated that was an end of the matter and that there would be no further discussion.

Mary managed to reassure some of the doubters by telling them she knew Tom Toulson and his family and was certain he would be an asset to the school. Miss Bramble's instincts proved to be well founded. Tom settled into the school without any problems, and quickly became accepted by most of the staff. The performance of the pupils in the GCE O and A levels remained at the same high level and even improved after a couple of years. Among other things, Tom became involved with the Portsmouth Physics Society, and on occasions arranged for girls in the Upper Sixth to attend some of the monthly evening talks at the Municipal College given by visiting lecturers.

During the winter of 1970 he took several of his charges to a lecture on 'Wormholes and the space-time continuum'. Despite the complexity of the mathematical equations that the lecturer wrote on the blackboard, it was a very interesting and illuminating lecture and the auditorium was filled with an enraptured audience. At the end of the lecture, as was the custom, the visiting professor invited those present if they had any questions. After he had answered all the questions from the auditorium floor, there were a handful of people who stayed behind with their own crackpot 'theories of relativity'. This evening was no different. He had quickly and efficiently disproved and invalidated five different ideas ranging from the semi-plausible to the downright ridiculous, when Tom, the last in the queue, came forward. Although the professor was keen to get away because he had a train to catch, he took the time to listen to all comments after his lecture. Tom explained how his father had been sorting out some old photographs that he'd taken when he was serving abroad in the RAF in the 1920s. One photo in particular puzzled him. It was one that he had taken when he was in Arabia. He'd written on the back of it 'a photograph of something that wasn't there – 1925'. Tom passed the photo to the professor.

'When I asked my Dad about it, he said that someone in the photography section suggested that the picture was probably the result of a mirage effect, but he had never been convinced by that explanation,' said Tom. 'He also said that it had been quite eerie when he took the snap because there was a complete absence of sound at the instant he operated the shutter.'

The professor took a cursory glance at the photo and handed it back to Tom.

'Yes, I expect it was something to do with a mirage, although I would have expected a more shimmering effect.' He was thinking, *'right, now I can go and catch my train,'* when suddenly he had a second thought. 'Hang on a minute – could I have another look at the photograph?'

Tom handed the photo back to him, and the professor took a magnifying glass out of his briefcase. After closely examining what looked like a blemish on the right hand side of the picture he said. 'That looks like a diffraction pattern. Could I keep this photograph for a little while so that I may discuss some aspects of it with my colleagues?'

Tom said that he could and gave him his name and school address.

'You don't have the negative, do you?'

'I'm afraid not – it's been long lost.'

The professor thanked him and went off to catch his train.

Tom didn't hear from the professor for over three months. When he did, he was intrigued by what he had to say. In the letter that accompanied the returned photograph, the professor said the photo had caused a division of opinion in his department. Nearly all accepted that the blemish was a diffraction pattern, and by using the size of the camels as a reference, the spacing of the lines in the pattern indicated that – according to Schwartzschild's equations – it was compatible with what could be expected when a wormhole appeared in the space-time continuum. This would produce areas of time-diffracted light. The professor went on to say that this could be a photograph of a different time, but that didn't necessarily mean that it was.

So the mystery was not solved. It also meant that Tom had to do a lot more reading about wormholes.

As he was reading the professor's letter he recalled his dad mentioning something about Eileen, saying that she also had taken a picture of something that wasn't there. So the next time he visited, he asked his dad to tell him again what Eileen had said. Back at school on the Monday, he chatted to Mary in the staffroom, hoping to find out more about the picture.

'Dad said that the last time that he saw Eileen she told him that she'd taken an odd photograph, just as he had done over 40 years before,' he said. 'It was at that place inland from Aden.'

'Marib?' asked Mary.

'Yes, that's it. Well it was that photograph taken by my dad that I showed to the professor after the lecture he gave last term at the Physics Society meeting.'

'Eileen spent almost two years in Aden after that, Tom,

before she was posted back to the UK.'

'When did she get married?'

'She hasn't yet found Mr Right, or so she says. I don't think she will ever get married. I suppose she is a bit like me. But unlike me, she always seems to want to be on the move. She was only in the UK for a year before she was sent off to Singapore. She arrived there just in time for the Malaysian Emergency, and she spent another two years there before returning to the UK to complete her commission. That was in 1960.'

'So she lives in the UK now?'

'No, four years after leaving the RAF she went to live in Rhodesia, but I don't think she's too happy out there. It was OK until the UDI a couple of years after she had just got settled, but because of the sanctions she's become really disillusioned, like all the ex-pats. I think she'd really like to come home.'

'Would you give her my best regards the next time that you write to her?'

'Why don't you write to her yourself, Tom? I'm sure that would cheer her up no end.'

Mary gave him Eileen's address, and a week later he wrote to her. In his letter, as well as bringing her up to date with what had been going on with the Toulson family, he wrote about what the professor had said about his dad's photograph. He asked if she still had her weird photograph and whether it had one of those blemishes on it.

In her reply, Eileen said that she still had the photograph, and that she'd carefully checked it, and sure enough – there was a small circular blemishes right in the middle. She would show it to him and his dad when they next met.

It was not to be. In a letter that Tom wrote to her over the Christmas period of 1973, with a heavy heart he had to tell her that his dad had died. This was a very painful time for Tom and his family. His mum and dad had been married for over forty-four years and the family had always been close-knit. In times of trouble, his dad had always been there as an anchor, sorting out any problems that arose. Tom realised that he would now have to take on that role ... but for now the family had to grieve.

Tom arranged for Margaret to move in with him and his wife. Although his mother was still quite able and agile, he knew

183

that with such a huge chunk taken out of her life, living on her own would be very lonely, very lonely indeed. The 'moving in' of Margaret into their household gave Tom an insight into the value of the 'ladies and mothers' club that Mary had established at the school twenty years earlier. Nevertheless it was a little while before things returned to any kind of normality.

To occupy himself during this period he returned to catching up with what was new in the field of wormhole theory. The more he read about them, the more he began to wonder. *'What if these were photographs of things and people trapped in wormholes in another time, like prehistoric insects trapped in solidified resin?'* This made him think about the possibility of other wormholes with people trapped in them. It was at this point that he started to speculate about people who had mysteriously disappeared, particularly after reading an article about the 'Marie Celeste'.

'How many wormholes had there been in the past? How many were there now? How big or small could they be? How many disappearances could be attributed to them? Were those trapped inside there for eternity? He came to the conclusion that they must be there forever. That is ... unless an event horizon coincided with ...'

Although it was all conjecture, he was to be brought dramatically back to speculating about ideas like these forty years later.

The morale of the white Rhodesians had reached an all-time low; the sanctions were making life more and more difficult, and the guerrilla incursions were becoming more frequent and more brutal. So, shortly after receiving Tom's letter, Eileen made up her mind to return to the UK. Because of the situation in Rhodesia she had to devise a complicated, slow and expensive route home. First she travelled to South Africa and then to West Africa, before taking a flight to Heathrow. Disastrously as it turned out, because a strike by BEA airport workers at Heathrow meant she ended up at Orly International airport in Paris on 3 March 1974. Her onward flight to Heathrow was cancelled and she was transferred to Flight 981, a Turkish Airlines DC10 on route from Istanbul to London. The aircraft crashed shortly after take-off killing all 346 passengers and crew.

This was a very sad time for Esme, Mary and Tom and their families. A few months after Mary had told her mum that Uncle Jack had died of a heart attack, she had to tell her that the baby of the family, Eileen, had been killed. After that, Esme was never quite the same again.

Her grief was not made any easier during the next twelve months, when two of the other mothers of the mothers-and-daughters group died within a few weeks of each other. Although the now reduced group continued to go out for their monthly afternoon teas, the conversations were never as enjoyable as they had been before.

Esme died in the last week of the 1975 spring term, a day before what would have been her eighty-fourth birthday, and Mary retired from teaching at the end of the summer term of that year after what she always referred to as the most fulfilling thirty years of her life.

The flat in Southsea was now too big for her, so she bought a one-bedroom apartment in the art deco block opposite where Lee Tower – now demolished – had once stood. Sometimes Tom would call by to see her, but apart from that she didn't have many visitors. Nevertheless she made quite a few friends and had a full and active life in the local community, and for three more decades life went on for Mary in the well-ordered fashion that she so liked.

It was over the Christmas period of 2011 that she became aware that she was beginning to forget things and frequently repeating what she had just said. She went to see her doctor and he confirmed that she had the onset of dementia.

'Mary, as you don't have any close family, you might want to consider moving into a warden controlled home, where they can keep an eye on you,' he said.

Always the sensible one, Mary took his advice, sold her apartment and moved into a care home in Lee, just before her ninety-third birthday in 2012. It was so comforting for her to have a nurse checking that everything was OK several times a day, and to have the doctor coming to see her every month.

Jennifer was the care nurse that Mary saw most often. She was a happy, rather plump young woman in her late twenties, well built rather than fat. There was another carer – Kate -who looked after Mary on Tuesday and Thursday mornings. One Tuesday afternoon when Kate was handing over to Jennifer, she said: 'Mary's been telling me her life story again this morning, quite a few times. She said that she was in the WRNS, but she couldn't tell me what she did because she had signed the official secrets act. I expect she was a cook.'

'No, Kate. I've seen some of her photographs – she was an officer.'

'Well she said that although she couldn't tell me about what she did in the WRNS, she could tell me something that would amaze me. She said she'd made a spring flow by striking a rock with a rod.'

'Ah, I haven't heard that one.'

'You will,' said Kate.

She was right. Jennifer did hear it, several times that day and on most days for about a week after that.

One of the things that Mary mentioned in her more lucid moments was that she used to visit a family in Raynes Road by the name of Toulson.

'Oh I live in Raynes Road, Mary,' said Jennifer. 'What was the number of the house where they lived?'

Mary looked blank. That was one of the things that her memory had lost.

Jennifer tended not to talk at home about what the residents in the nursing home said to her, but she did mention to her mum and dad the bit about the Toulsons. Several days later her mum said to her: 'You won't believe this, but I was talking to her next door this morning and she said that the Toulsons used to live in this house over 40 years ago.'

❦

Back during World War II, when the Wren that mum and dad knew had come to see them and he had been able to find that old rattling stone, Tom had been rather pleased with himself. So much so that he had decided to give the stone a permanent home. He'd taken it from the shed and jammed it on the corner of the concrete path which led from the back garden. Then he had fished out some old sand and cement from the shed, made up what he thought was the correct mix and cemented the stone onto the side of the path. Unfortunately, he hadn't thought through the idea properly, for although he was then able to show everyone where the stone was, no-one would have been able to rattle it. It had also become apparent that he was never going to be much of a builder because he had cemented the stone so that it stood proud of the path. This meant that every time a bike was wheeled from the shed in the back garden along the side of the house to the front gate it had bounced over the stone. His dad had not been too pleased with his efforts and moving that 'ruddy stone' had become one of those jobs that was always going to be done but never was. Consequently the stone had become progressively more polished as the years passed, until eventually no-one noticed that it was there.

The rattling stone that Jack had left with the family in Sheffield ended up with Cissy's grandson. He had not moved far from the family roots and lived with his wife in Kilnhurst, a small village just the other side of Rotherham. He was coming up for retirement and had always been a compulsive hoarder. The stone had eventually found itself a cosy little obscure 'home' in the crowded attic of the magpie's semi-detached house.

One of the Nursing Sister colleagues of Eileen – the one who'd found the rattling stone when the group had visited Marib – rediscovered it over sixty years later when she was sorting out the junk in the loft shortly after her husband had died. For some reason that she could never really fathom, her husband had kept her 'trophy' for all those years. In fact she'd wondered why she had even bothered to bring it back at all. She should have thrown it away years ago. As she'd sat on an old suitcase in the loft, with the single low-wattage light bulb above her head for company, she had started thinking about her life and how she would have to manage now that her husband had gone before her. It wasn't going to be easy, but she'd always known that she was reasonably well provided for, as long as she didn't go on too many spending sprees. She had sadly reflected about her husband's death. The grim reaper never comes on a convenient day or at a convenient time, but to come a'calling on the day before their Golden Wedding anniversary had seemed a bit ill-timed.

Absentmindedly shaking the stone, she had decided that rather than just throwing it in the bin she would take the curiosity to a small business in town that dealt with semi-precious stones and geological samples – the proprietor had been a friend of her late husband and one of the intended guests at what would have been their anniversary celebration.

'Sorry to hear about Colin,' he'd said. 'It was so sudden. How are you coping?'

'OK, Bob – of course I miss him and the house seems so quiet, but I'm managing alright.'

The normal pleasantries had continued for a while. Then she'd asked him if he could tell her anything about the stone that she had found near Aden when she was a young Nursing Sister.

She had handed him the stone. He'd looked at it, done the compulsory rattling, and said: 'Well I've never seen anything quite like it before, but it could have a quartz interior. If you like, I could cut it in half with my diamond cutter to see what makes it rattle, but if I do that's the end of its rattling days.'

'You might as well, Bob,' she'd said. 'People very soon lose interest in it after a couple of shakings.'

Jennifer was sitting watching the television news at lunchtime while she had a snack before going on duty at the care home. An item came on that attracted her attention. She called her mum to come in and watch it. Introducing the story, the presenter said: 'Here is a piece of happy news. A recently widowed ex-RAF Nursing Sister has had an unexpected windfall. When she was sorting out the bric-a-brac in her loft she discovered that she still had a 'rattling stone' that she'd brought home from Aden over fifty years ago. When she had the stone cut open it was found to contain a ruby the size of a hen's egg, and it's been valued at over a million pounds.'

'Lucky beggar eh, Mum? Makes you want to go to Aden to have a look for one yourself, but knowing my luck it would be a wasted journey.'

Jennifer finished her lunch, went and got her bike from the shed and cycled off to the care home.

That afternoon when she was giving Mary her tea she mentioned the news item about the ruby. Mary looked up.

'I used to have a rattling stone,' she said, 'but I gave it to a museum.'

'Of course you did, Mary,' said Jennifer in a condescending tone that was completely missed by Mary. 'Was that when you were in the WRNS?'

'No, I can't tell you what I did when I was a Wren, but when I was little I had a staff and when I struck a rock with it, I made a stream start.'

'Of course you did, Mary.'

'It was then that I had a rattling stone. Well, really it belonged to my brother Brian.'

'Of course it did, Mary.'

It was not that Jennifer was an unkind or uncaring person – on the contrary, she was very kind and caring by nature, but having conversations with the residents was always quite difficult.

A few days later Jennifer arrived home in a very distraught state.

'What's the matter, Jen?' her mum asked.

'It's Mary, mum – she's gone.'

'There there, dear. She was 94 and she had that dementia – she's better off now. No-body lives forever.'

'No, I don't mean she's died – she's just gone.'

'What do you mean, love, "just gone"?'

'The people at the care home said that somehow early this morning, just before it was light, she got dressed and managed to slip out of the back door. They informed the police and although a lot of people have been looking for her everywhere, there's no sign of her.'

'Don't worry, Jen, she'll turn up.'

She didn't.

That evening on the local television news there was a report on Mary's disappearance in which they interviewed a local man who had reported seeing Mary that morning. He lived in Skipper Way, about half a mile from the seafront, and had recently retired and was in the habit of taking his dog for a walk every morning.

'I'm just recovering from a knee operation, and I like to take the dog for his walk because it helps me with my recuperation,' he said.

He went on to explain how he took the dog in the back of his car to the Elmore car park, let his dog out and then walked across to the steps that lead down to the promenade.

'We always go the same way, down the steps, along the little part of the promenade and on to Browndown ranges. Scruff loves it there – plenty of room for him to run about – and I like to go early to watch the sun come up.

'Anyhow, I'd just got to the top of the steps and Scruff was already at the bottom when I noticed an old lady walking along the promenade, towards the ranges. I wasn't worried about Scruff because he never bothers people, but I knew that something was wrong because although the elderly lady was fully dressed and wearing a coat, she only had her slippers on. I called out to her to ask if everything was alright, but she didn't hear me. I didn't worry because I knew that I would soon catch up with Scruff and her once I got to the bottom of the steps. The knee operation means that I have to take my time going down steps. I only stopped for about half a minute to look in the opposite direction at one of the new cruise liners that was coming out of Southampton. When I reached the bottom few steps the sun was just appearing and I was suddenly aware of a very creepy silence … but it only seemed to last for a few moments. I walked down to the start of the ranges but I couldn't see Scruff or the elderly lady. I called and called and called him, but Scruff and the lady in her slippers had just disappeared. I spent over an hour looking for them without any joy. Then I came home and phoned the police.'

At the beginning of the summer of 2014, the brook that had flowed across the top corner of four acre field for as long as anyone could remember, dried up.

🍃 🍃 🍃